Rainer Bressler, retired lawyer and writer, born in 1945, is Swiss and lives in Zurich. From 1980 to 1993 he distinguished himself as an author of radioplays.

Publications to date:

7 Radioplays:
Tom Garner und Jamie Lester; Morgenkonzert; Folgen Sie mir, Madame; Aufruhr in Zürich; Nächst der Sonne; Geliebter / Geliebte; Gaukler der Nacht; Beinahe-Minuten-Krimi
Produced and broadcast by Swiss radio SRF between 1979 and 1993

Published Books:
Geliebter / Geliebte. 8 Hörspiele, Karpos Verlag, Loznica 2008
Privatzeug 1856 bis 2012. Versuch einer Spurensuche, 5 Bände:
Spur 1 Reisen; Spur 2 Spielen; Spur 3 Schreiben; Spur 4 Dichten; Spur 5 Weben
BoD 2012 bis 2016
Pink Champagne, satirischer Roman, BoD 2020
Schattenkämpfe, Roman, BoD 2020
Gärung, satirischer Roman, BoD 2020
Reise-Impressionen, Reiseberichte, BoD 2020
Kraut & Rüben, Kurzgeschichten, BoD 2020
Texturen, satirischer Roman, BoD 2020
Theaterstücke, Band 1-3, BoD 2020
Fenstersturz, Krimi-Satire, BoD 2021

Rainer Bressler

Shadow Fight(s)

Rough translation from the German by
Denise Uebersax

Originally published in German as „Schattenkämpfe" by
BoD, Norderstedt (Germany) in 2020

Rough translation: Denise Uebersax

www.rainerbressler.ch

Cover: Rainer Bressler: Untitled, Textile and Painted Iron
Wire, 1971; Foto Rainer Bressler

The stories told in the novel are based on real events and real
people. The real places and names of the persons are used in
the novel. Nevertheless, in the interest of intimate vividness
beyond biographical facts, the plot and drawing of the events
and characters of the persons are freely invented and
fictitious.

Production and publishing: BoD – Books on Demand,
Norderstedt (Germany)

ISBN: 978-3-755716709

Bibliografische Information der Deutschen
Nationalbibliothek:
Die Deutsche Nationalbibliothek verzeichnet diese
Publikation in der Deutschen Nationalbibliografie;
detaillierte bibliografische Daten sind im Internet über
http://dnb.dnb.de abrufbar.

A YOUNG GERMAN IN SWITZERLAND IN 1937

1.

Shortly after midnight in the moonlight on a clear night that could not be more idyllic, an elegant limousine floats as it were silently on 19 October 1937 over a pretty sleepy thoroughfare lined with pretty family homes through an orderly bourgeois-looking outer district of the Swiss capital Bern. Chauffeur S. drives his boss, Professor K., chief doctor of the "Heil- und Pflegeanstalt" (Psychiatric University Hospital) Waldau, from Bern's main railway station back to the hospital, popularly known as the loony bin.

K. returns home from a visit to a psychiatric congress in Berlin on a train that arrived punctually at a late hour in Bern. S., if he is to live up to his reputation as a reliable chauffeur and survive as K.'s chauffeur, must be on hand despite the unusual working hours.

K.'s presentation had deeply impressed his German colleagues, as had been pointed out to him several times. They had showered him with praise. K. is not aware of the fears that have recently arisen among some Swiss colleagues about working with German colleagues. He rejoices that this cooperation is highly profitable for him. The fact, that certain colleagues here turn up their noses at his behaviour, does not bother him. So they don't get in his way in the professional exchange with Germany. He survives gloriously in the tough professional competition. He benefits from an outstanding position in Germany. K. likes the

Germans' brash, somewhat full-bodied and clearly determined manner.

S. slows down the limousine. K. abruptly wakes up from his thoughts. Straightening up on his back seat in the limousine. Looking out of the back of the limousine through the windscreen over S.'s shoulder into the darkness, approaching them not quite so dark. With shadowy outlines of the trunks and treetops of the avenue trees. Appearing ghostly in this light. S. steers the vehicle at walking pace, from the thoroughfare into the park area of the clinic. The avenue is the dead straight access road to the park of the clinic. To the imposing main building in neoclassical style. Which can be seen in the distance.

The park also contains, in addition to the huge main building, the other hospital buildings for the patients, the farm buildings and stables, the stately home of K. and his family, as well as buildings with flats and rooms for the medical staff and other employees of the clinic.

S. is alert. In the cone of the spotlight, in the middle of the now brightly lit part of the avenue, halfway to the main building, a tightly intertwined tangle of people emerges, clearly recognizable in the glare of the light. Instantly, the tangle breaks free from the conflation and becomes a woman staring terrified into the light and a man also staring terrified into the light. The two of them immediately scurry to the edge of the headlights, from the middle of the path to the edge by the tree trunks. They give way to the car. S. recognizes the two. Both employees of the clinic. The spontaneous joy at knowing about the relationship of the two, he has now caught, gives way to the equally spontaneous uncertainty whether the boss has also seen and recognized them clearly. Which could end fatally for the two of them. S. spontaneously slows down. He is about to drive past the two now standing in the almost dark on the left of the car.

„Blimey, the darn foreigner and that silly tramp, who falls for his smooching.", S. presses out. Barely audibly, but with a clearly perceptible ironic undertone. He pretends his remark to be a soliloquy. On purpose. In reality he parodies the boss's pejorative phrase, recently picked up with genuine irritation. He now gleefully confronts the boss with his loose saying. That is stuck in his, S.'s, memory. S. knows, Doctor B. is thoroughly okay and a good chap. Although he is a German. The always cheerful nurse Hedy is a most attractive and beautiful woman. S. himself wouldn't mind, to have a date with her. He envies Doctor B. for his luck with women. Women think, it's smarter to flirt with a slick German doctor than with an uncouth little Swiss chauffeur and gofer at the clinic. He is surprised that the two of them, who, unlike other employees, always arrive on time for work in the morning, now only come home from partying in town at such a late hour.

K. is annoyed by the impertinent and out-of-place remark by chauffeur S.. How come, he dares to mimic him, the boss. How dare S. take a joking remark by his boss out of context and provocatively repeat it as a reproach. K. notices the two figures startled in the cone of dim light. He also recognizes the two culprits. Annoyed at their impudence in being caught red-handed in public. Where he, K., the boss, had clearly forbidden B., who himself is merely a temporary trainee among the doctors of the cliic, to have a flirtation with a nurse at the clinic.

Only a few days or weeks ago, on the occasion of a social dance event of the staff in the clinic, K. had caught B. clearly overstepping the boundaries of decency and ignoring with a grin the rules of the clinic in front of everyone. In dancing lasciviously and demonstratively socialising as a doctor of the clinic with a nurs of the clinic, this silly tramp. K. had taken B. aside, not without causing a small commotion. B. was told in no uncertain terms, that love affairs between doctors of the clinic and nurses of the clinic were strictly forbidden. Should B., as a minor intern, dare to violate this rule again, he would have to leave the clinic immediately. Which meant the end of his internship at the clinic. Which he, K., had had granted to him out of pure philanthropy. He, K., would then also no longer be available to him as a doctoral supervisor. B.'s future is none of K.'s concerns. Having joineded the festivities again after having reprimanded B., K. boasted laughingly to his chauffeur S. in public, that he had really put the 'darn foreigner' in his place for fooling around with 'that silly tramp who, falls for his smooching'.

Let these young people have their fun elsewhere, but not in his, K.'s, kingdom. Here cleanliness, correctness and decency must prevail. This cheeky monkey of B. seems to be out, to get in the way of him, K., on whom he is still dependent as a doctoral student and subordinate. Unbelieveable how this rogue dares to behave! Such good-for-nothings who have 'fallen off the devil's wagon' have no place in his clinic. K. does not understand how he could have fallen of all people for this guy, who by chance happens to be

German. K. is outraged. Now definitely an alarm bell rings and it is high time to …

K. gleefully seeks revenge. In a moment, the limousine will glide past the two, who have stepped aside into the darkness on the left in front of the tree trunks. K. turns his head to the left. Shoots his sparrowhawk glance out through the side window on the left. And sure enough, in a fraction of a second, the terrified grimace of B., staring stunned into the interior of the limousine, lights up. K. triumphs. B. must leave the clinic at once and for good. With a proper and heavy thrashing, that he will remember for his lifetime.

Doubts and fears make K.'s joy fade away. He absolutely must keep his composure and be strict. In front of B.. In front of S.. In fornt of the whole staff of his clinic. He has to show, what a tough man he is. At the same time he must avoid, to involuntarily cause new damage. Diplomacy and tact are required. To plan his further steps, he has to make sure, that the news about the two culprits spreads by tomorrow morning among the whole staff of the clinic. And his strict reacting at people who break the rules must be known by his staff. His reputation as a boss, who can't be fooled and who relies on morals and decency and punishes wrongdoers severely but consistently, is to be confirmed. Therefore he has to induce S. to be his perfect messenger and his willing tool. For this purpose he mumbles, astonishingly loud and clear, given as if it were a soliloquy, to the address of S.,"the conceited B. will get a serious thrashing, just he wait!' It is still incomprehensible to K., how he had been deceived by B. in such a way.

About a year ago a German colleague he knew from a conference in Berlin had asked him, if he would be willing to be doctoral supervisor at the University of Bern for a young German. This young man has his degree from the the medical faculty of the universitiy in Breslau. But he has not yet written his dissertation. He needs to write it, to get the finishing touch for his doctoral hat. To grant the young man at the same time an of course unpaid traineeship at the Waldau University Clinic for the duration of his dealings with the dissertation at the University of Bern. So he can get in touch with psychiatry. K. had been flattered, that his reputation had apparently reached as far as Germany. A young German even coveted him as a doctoral supervisor. From which K. concluded that the young German must be an exceptional student. Seven months were agreed upon. May, up to and including November 1937. ‚And now, in October, this awful surprise', K. sighs.

For the time being, B. had turned out to be a basically ordinary guy. Of small stature, slim and agile. Pays a lot of attention to his appearance. Always correct and well-dressed. And well-groomed. At first sight he seems inquisitive, of the best manners, extremely polite. B. is effusively enthusiastic about the topic K. proposes to him as a doctoral thesis. "Kinder im Wahnsystem der Mutter" (Children in the mother's delusional system). B. never stops emphasizing how interested he is in this very subject. K. regards B.'s ingratiating remark to his doctoral supervisor as somewhat aloof and improper. Then B. doesn't stop pretending, how happy he is, to have found in him, the honored Professor K., a mentor who is famous in professional circles and who has a wide range of interests. "If I have understood correctly, you, Professor, are writing poetry and theatre plays as wll, just like I do." A few days later B. asks K., his professor   and doctoral supervisor, if it were not advisible, to expand the topic to "Kinder im Wahnsystem der Eltern" (Children in the parents' delusional system). K. must admit, that B.'s suggestion makes sense and approves to it. But in B.'s style is too much unseemly familiarity and lack of distance. K.'s gut feeling tells him, that he won't be happy about this student. Has got himself into a tough situation with this young man. This feeling is strengthened more and more as the days and weeks go by. Somehow and unwillingly he even is impressed by B.'s snappy cutting and his snappy manner. He is so diffrent from the locals. K. notices, how B. turns out to be in private a epicure, seeking pleasures, wherever poissible, and a dsarling of the ladies. He developed to be the darling of everyone. A dazzler, a polished lacquer monkey, who carries his humanistic education in front of him like a placard. And yet, despite all his zeal, a good-for-nothing and a show-off. K. realizes that B. has two faces. A seemingly serious face, which in its exaggerated seriousness becomes a farce, as it were, when he stands opposite him, K.. And a laughing face when he feels unobserved by his highest superior. And now, even after a warning, again this incident with this nurse. A brazen violation of a strict rule, that had been brought clearly to his attention.

As curious as K. is about B.'s networking in Breslau and Berlin with German luminaries in the field of psychiatry, the latter always keeps a low profile about his actual relationships. Wimps him, K., grinning cheekily with evasive answers and ironic remarks. K. must conclude from this, that B. is not connected to important professional circles in Berlin or Breslau. K. also has to admit to himself, that his willingness to take this young man on as a doctoral student and as a trainee in his clinic, turns out as a mistake. If K. now, as would be absolutely right, throws B. out of the clinic and refuses to be any longer his doctoral supervisor, there would come up a problem. B.'s doctoral thesis must soon be completed. B. would get most angry about K.'s acting. Probably he would after his prematurely return home badmouth him in Breslau and Berlin. As K. ist not absolutely sure, if B. doesn't have after all some connections to important German psychiatric circles, B.'s outrage could gnaw on K.'s reputation in Berlin and Breslau. Which would be fatal for K.. K. must avoid this risk at all costs. The new situation requires a subtle approach. If, contrary to expectations, B.'s doctoral thesis turns out not to be totally flawed, K. will have the advantage of waving it through with a top grade. But B. must not get away without a good thrashing for his cheeky provocation and impropriety. A kick in his backside. Then sent back to from whence he came. Sent back as a sample of no value. The senior doctor, under whom B. works, must carry out B.'s thrashing! K. will give strict instructions to this senior doctor.

These thoughts flash through K.'s head in a split second, while his gaze is directed out the window to the left to gaze at the culprit and his playmate for a brief moment in the gloom through the side window from the back of the limousine as they pass. Sure enough, B.'s noggin whizzes by with a bewildered expression on its face, staring into the dark rear of the limousine. K. has seen B. And B. seems to have perceived him, K.!

In the dark rear of the limousine, which glides past him and Hedy with a low hum, Hans Günther B. catches the face and the piercingly evil gaze of K., who is enthroned stiffly like a cardboard companion in the interior of the limousine. Hans Günther's teeth and all his limbs spontaneously chatter. The thought, darn it, it's all over now, flashes into Hans Günther's consciousness with a proper after-flicker. In a fraction of a second, he senses the catastrophe. The immediate expulsion. The failure with his dissertation. The hardest work during the last months here in Bern - all for nothing! The beautiful dream of professional success as a doctor in Breslau or Berlin, of marriage to his Uschi in Breslau and of the eagerly awaited offspring, who must be named Rainer in honour of Rilke, the poet colleague. Hans Günther spontaneously flashes the thought that only now, in retrospect, does he recognize the relationship between him and his doctoral supervisor and boss as having been a constant shadow fight since the beginning, which will now slide into an open fight.

A hand - a female hand - touches Hans Günther. Warmth trickles through his body, which had previously frozen into a block of ice at the perception of K.'s mask-like grimace. The touch of the warming hand and the subsequent embrace, which he returns only too gladly and hotly, melt all ice. The bliss is sealed with a never-ending succession of the hottest kisses. In the middle of the avenue leading to the main building of the clinic. On this glorious autumn night with a full moon, 19 October 1937.

When he starts work the next morning, Hans Günther is ordered by K.'s secretary to see his senior doctor without delay. Hans Günther is frightfully agitated. He gets on very well with his senior doctor. But this time he must act on K.'s command. Hans Günther fears the worst. That this senior doctor, who is usually easy-going and most friendly, will have to adress him this time in an entirely different tune. Already in the corridor in front of the senior doctor's office, Hans Günther comes across him. He approaches his senior doctor with his eyes downcast. Hoping that the terrible moment will soon be over.

The senior doctor holds Hans Günther with brute force. Shakes him vigorously. Until Hans Günther looks up at him. Then the senior doctor lets go of Hans Günther. He poses opposite Hans Günther. He puts on a stern, bitterly angry face. Like Hans Günther has never seen on him before. Hans Günther begs heaven for a smooth landing. The senior doctor begins to wave his right hand, clenched in a fist, and his extended index finger in front of Hans Günther's face. As he does so, he utters in a threatening voice, "Oh dear! Mei, mei, mei." (In Swiss dialect this sequence of syllables is an exclamation of threat, but sounds as if three times the month of May were pronounced!) Hans Günther suspects that something is not quite right. That the senior doctor is suppressing laughter at his threatening gesture. That the exaggerated threat is just an act. Hans Günther is already so familiar with the idiom of his host country and specifically with the Swiss dialect that he understands the threatening content of the to him otherwise meaningless syllable sequence of 'mei mei mei'. Spontaneously, he plays dumb.

"If Mister Senior Doctor allows me the remark, we are no longer in the merry month of May. It is already October!"

They both burst out laughing. With furtive glances to the left and right, the senior doctor resumes a serious posture. Hans Günther does the same.

"You know very well that, as a doctor at the clinic, it is strictly forbidden for you to have a love affair with a nurse at the clinic. One more time and you will experience the worst. The boss has instructed me to give you a good thrashing. You've been warned," the senior doctor says in a stern, firm, loud voice, then whispers to Hans Günther, "so now I've carried out the boss' order and reprimanded you. Please don't get caught next time. A little more discretion. Watch out, boss approaching! Mime a beaten dog."

The senior doctor lets his gaze dart discreetly in the direction from whence danger is in the suit.

Hans Günther snorts briefly and then goes up to K. in a humble posture and smiling. Stooping to indicate that he has something to say to him.

"If you wish to address the vexed matter, don't bother. The senior doctor will have clarified it for you, what decency and a sense of honour require of a budding doctor."

"Professor, you are right as usual. I was going to ask you for an appointment. I have finished my thesis and would like to deliver it to you."

"Get an appointment from my secretary. Anything else? I'm in a hurry."

Hans Günther lets out a sigh of relief. Lucky him. The whole thing has gone off without a hitch. As he considers this, the thought flashes spontaneously: And what will happen to Hedy? He thinks in horror that she, poor thing, is at the mercy of the head nurse's sanctions and will certainly not know how to defend herself. He is so ashamed that he has put poor Hedy in such a situation. On the spur of the moment, he rushes into town to buy a box of confectionery for Hedy. On the way to town in the bus, he scribbles with his Pelikan fountain-pen on a piece of paper the mini-poem that had occurred to him on waking up. Now suddenly it comes back to his memory. He can write it down from his mind. ‚O Psychiater junger / lass ab vom Liebeshunger / zur holden Schwesternschaft / es könnten sonst wir Alten / nicht mit euch Tempo halten / drum opfert euch der Wissenschaft!' (O psychiatrist, young / Let go of your hunger for love / To the fair sisterhood / Otherwise we old people / Could not keep up with you, / So sacrifice yourself to science!). Hans Günther hopes that no one at the clinic will notice his brief absence. He buys a pretty box of confectionery in the confectionery shop. He sticks the note with the verse on top of it.

Back in the clinic, as soon as the coast is clear, Hans Günther sneaks into a hidden place from which he can spot Hedy and Hedy him. Discreetly, he beckons her to come to him. To his astonishment, Hedy is amused. She is delighted with the box of confectionery. Gives Hans Günther a slap on the right cheek as a thank you and playfully reproaches him, "You are mean, you want me to get fat!" Then they spontaneously fall into each other's arms. Only to part again with furtive glances around. Hedy contorts her mouth into a grin.

"The head nurse's scolding clarified for me, that I don't need to feel guilty about quitting my job at the Waldau. I was spot on with my resignation some time ago. The fact, that she now tried to finish me off again, is ridiculous. Congratulate me on my new job at the Bircher Benner Clinic in Zurich!"

Hans Günther, who had just been so elated, is knocked off his feet by the words Hedy throws at him. He no longer knows what to think. His lover had kept the most important things from him for days or weeks.

"Don't look so horrified! Zurich is not out of this world. Visit me in Zurich."

Hans Günther doesn't brood for long. He whispers in Hedy's ear, "I'll be with you in Zurich every free minute. Just you wait!"

Hedy pushes him away, laughing.

"I have to get back! And thank you for the confectionery."

"And hopefully also for the verse, so prettily composed especially for you."

"Oh yes."

Hans Günther hates to be overwhelmed by new developments that he had imagined differently. Of course, he had had no specific ideas about his relation to Hedy. With her, he enjoys the moment. But now, that she will leave for Zurich, what he only learns by chance, and she has kept this decision from him for a long time, he has to question the carefree familiarity that has prevailed between them until now. His trust in Hedy is shaken. Fortunately, he still has his fiancée Uschi in Breslau, about whom he never had talked to Hedy. She is waiting for him there. Whom, he now will not have to face with the accomplished fact of a separation, as he had feared, if his relation with Hedy would have got really serious. He is delighted that he will soon have his doctorate in his pocket and can finally run away home. He had already passed the oral doctoral examination at the University of Bern in the summer. His trainee position at the Waldau expires at the end of next month. In the next few days, he will hand in his finished doctoral thesis to K.. Everything will be wrapped up by the end of the year. And he will be happy at home, in the arms of his flame Uschi in Breslau, whom he will marry as soon as possible and with whom he will beget the longingly awaited son and heir named Rainer.

Wolfgang F. invites Hans Günther to the Kursaal to celebrate his doctorate. F. has made it. And the whole stress with the disseratation lies behind him. A Hungarian ladies' band plays lively tunes in the Kursaal.

Like Hans Günther, F. is from Breslau. Hans Günther had not known him at home. F. is the son of friends of Mottl and Vatel, Hans Günther's parents. He had come to Bern to do his doctorate in pharmacy. Mottl had told Hans Günther that the son of friends, Wolfgang F., was also doing his doctorate in Berne and had given Hans Günther his address. So that they would not be completely lost in a foreign country, it would be nice if they could keep in touch, which would make both their parents happy. Hans Günther does not feel lost in Bern at all. Since the beginning of his stay in Berne, he has had very pleasant contact with his colleagues at the Waldau. But is always curious about new acquaintances. F. turns out to be a fussy, correct type. From time to time, they meet in dance clubs to get to know the local wine and the Bernese girls.

Now Hans Günther and F. sit together in the Kursaal with Blauburgunder wine and fiery sounds of the Hungarian women's band.

"And just imagine, B., I have already been accepted for a job in a pharmacy. In Shanghai. Next week I'll travel to Marseille, and then I'll steam off to faraway China.

My fiancée at home has also found a job in Shanghai independently of me. She will be joining me in a few months. Am I not a lucky man?"

Hans Günther congratulates F. effusively, although he would cross himself not to be able to work in Germany and to plan his future elsewhere. Moreover, he feels that fleeing abroad, especially in such times, is cowardice. Nevertheless, he raises his glass and toasts F. to a happy future.

"And what about your thesis, B.?"

"Next week I have an appointment with Professor K., my boss, and I will press the completed thesis into his hands and be back home by the end of the year! In the arms of my beloved Uschi, who is waiting for me in Breslau. We will get married, have children and lead a leisurely life. Yes, yes, F., that's just how different plans and life concepts are."

Hans Günther notices that F. is puzzled. He, the conservative conformist, is probably a little confused, Hans Günther thinks, that in addition to Hedy and others, there is suddenly talk of a lover in Breslau. To his relief, F. does not mention his polygamy. Which does not surprise him. He and F. are not that intimate, after all. F. starts an exclamation of horror.

"Back home, B.? Are you out of your mind! The political developments there, our poor professional prospects there ..."

"Doctors are always needed, thank God! Also and especially in our homeland, where it is important to show that our heart still beats for the good of Germany, the land of poets and thinkers, our homeland," Hans Günther throws out and then adds with a laugh, "by the time I return home to the Reich, Hitler and the National Socialists will have long been history. Don't look at me with such astonishment. My curiosity and my instinct to look closely always show me a way out of every mess. Anyway, I feel like throwing in the towel with my doctorate and following my true vocation. To devote myself to writing. But I can't do that to my old man. He wants me to wear a doctoral hat. Without a doctorate, I'm no good to him."

Punctual as a perfectly ticking clock, Hans Günther arrives at Professor K.'s secretary's office two minutes before the agreed time for the meeting. K. keeps Hans Günther waiting for ten minutes. Beaming, with a bend, Hans Günther hands K. the typescript of his doctoral thesis. K. accepts the thick bundle of paper. Moves it back and forth. Looks at it. His face is puckered.

"Fine, your doctoral thesis. Thank you. The scope is huge, almost too huge."

Hans Günther listens up. K.'s usual condescending tone has a mocking, derogatory undertone today. Hans Günther suspects that something is fishy with this noble Professor K.. Hans Günther had been lately looking through several dissertations by other persons. Several of those were as extensive as his. Or even longer with many more pages.

"Allow me, Professor, to mention, that the topic you suggested to me, which I worked my way into with full interest, has so much in it."

"Until I have fought my way through it! Gosh, it will take time! B., you can't expect a report from me before the end of the year. Your internship here at the clinic will end in a month. Then you will be a free man. Enjoy the time untill I give you notice, that I am through with your manuscript."

Hans Günther swallows empty. He had imagined the conversation with K., which is most important for him, differently. He is dismayed. And he is amazed at how quickly he is being led out of the lion's den. In this case he will return home in November and has later to come back to Bern to have the final talks with K. about his dissertation and get the confirmation paper of his successfully made degree. He will forget Hedy, with a tear in his eye. At home, he will renew his love for Uschi. Uschi as the mother of his planned son Rainer is also totally okay. At home, he can take his time to see what doors and gates will open for him professionally with a doctor's hat. If all else fails, he will devote himself entirely to writing and intellectual life, much to the dismay of Mottl and Vatel. Hans Günther informs his parents that he will be returning home at the beginning of December and will then go on a short trip to Bern at the end of this year or beginning of next year to deal with all the final formalities of his degree from the Bern University.

Hans Günther and Hedy celebrate Hedy's departure from Bern and the abrupt end of their oh so fine love affair with champagne and dancing in the bar of the Bellevue Palace Hotel. Hans Günther is annoyed that he had not brought his evening suit from home in his luggage for this so dignified occasion. He is ashamed of his knickerbocker suit in this elegant atmosphere. Hedy says, 'screw it, come on, come on, dance now!' They celebrate exuberantly. Hans Günther is blissful and enjoys the moment.

Mottl and Vatel implore Hans Günther in writing not to dare show up at home without his doctor's hat in his luggage. They bombard him with postcards and letters every day. Hans Günther pauses. It is not usually Mottl and Vatel's style to pester him so much. There must be something behind it that they don't want to - or can't / aren't allowed to – write in a letter. The postal censorship! In a postscript, they add that Germany's foreign exchange office no longer approves money transfers to him in Switzerland after his unpaid traineeship at the clinic expires. Hans Günther's breath catches in his throat. He is sure that Mottl and Vatel are not sending out these alarm signals for no reason.

Hans Günther sees himself at the mercy of the situation. Willy-nilly, he has to hold out in Bern, in Switzerland, until he gets the proper document of his successful doctoral graduation. His parents cannot continue to support him financially. Now he has to see for himself, how he will survive financially for at least one or maybe two more months in Switzerland. He could tear his hair out one by one for not having managed more carefully with the monthly remittances from his parents, he had received up until now. The remittance had been higher than a regular assistant's salary. Why had he squandered his money! Unexpectedly, he is catapulted out of a comfortable situation.

Hans Günther is not at a loss for a solution to his current problems. After all, he knows what he wants. And he is prepared to fight for it. Meanwhile, he has noticed that psychiatric clinics in Switzerland tend to have difficulties recruit young Swiss doctors as assistant doctors. He will jump into a vacancy. At the same time, he will earn a decent income. He doesn't need to tell a possible future employer that he's just staying in Switzerland until he's got his doctorate under his belt. He finds out about all the psychiatric clinics in Switzerland. He writes to all of them. He sends them his application papers. He receives rejection after rejection. The end of November, when his trainee position at the Waldau Clinic expires, is already awfully close. Hans Günther laughs and tells his colleagues from there, that if all else fails, he will run away to Paris, pretend to be a Belarusian nobleman and take a job as a chauffeur.

Finally, finally, a request to introduce himself in person. To the head doctor of the Cantonal Psychiatric Clink Königsfelden. If all else so far has failed, this time it will work out, for real! Hans Günther gets the picture of Königsfelden: A ducal monastery founded in 1306 by the Habsburg family on the site of a Roman garrison town, Vindonissa. A chequered history, and today even a loony bin.

It works! Hans Günther gets a regular job as an assistant doctor. He does not say a word to the head doctor of the Königsfelden Clinic, that he will leave for Breslau as soon as he has got his doctoral hat from the University of Bern. He starts at the Königsfelden Clinic on 1 December 1937. Königsfelden lies between Bern and Zurich. Closer to Zurich. From now on regular wages seamlessly replace the dwindling financial support from Mottl and Vatel. Hans Günther is saved for the moment. Smiles at the idea that Mottl will write, once again, you're so lucky. You're just a Sunday child. He'll stay in Switzerland for another while. He'll be closer to Hedy and have fun with her as often as possible in Zurich. And console himself with her over everything unpleasant. But soon, soon he will head back to the Reich!

2.

Edwin F. hears the knock on his office door. Glances at his wristwatch to make sure it is half past 11 a.m.. Calls in and knows that the door is about to open and the postman, Paul O., will hand him the incoming lunchtime mail for the staff of the clinic. Edwin F. hopes, that this time Paul O. has not been stopped again at the entrance gatehouse to the Königsfelden Clinic and the park by the young orderly for the first time on duty as porter. As had been the case in the morning, when Paul O. had delivered the morning mail. Paul O. had been stopped to show his authorization to enter the clinic grounds. As Windisch's postman in his smart uniform, Paul O. needs no further authorization. The young man should learn that.

Paul O. puts a pile of letters on Edwin F.'s desk and says with a laugh, that the young orderly on porter duty had learned his lesson well. Hats off! This time, the moment he perceived Paul O. turn onto the forecourt in front of the entrance gate from Zürcherstrasse on his bicycle, he immediately ran to open the gate. So that he, Paul O., did not even have to stop his bicycle, let alone get off it. As a postman, he had an official duty and had no time to idle away. He absolutely needed a clear path to the Königsfelden Administration Building. Even when the entrance to the park is forbidden for ordinary mortals. That's why ordinary people from the village and the region had named the loony bin the Monastery, pronounced with a definitely depreciating tone. A name referring to the historical, long-ago funtion of the area.

"By the way, Edi, do you know this Doctor Hans Günther B.? He often gets letters, apparently private correspondence, from all over the world. From Germany, from Venezuela, from Colombia, from Australia, from Rhodesia, from England, from Canada, from the USA. With great postal stamps. Can't we ask him, if he would be willing to swap these great stamps, or individual stamps ...?"

Edwin F. waves it off. He sees this specific doctor as well as all the other doctors of the clinic almost every day, when handing them their incoming mail in their offices. But asking a doctor something so personal was out of the question for him as a simple office clerk in the Königsfelden administration. On the other hand, he had heard from someone that this Doctor B. had been seen at the Stamp Exchange of the local Stamp Association in Baden. So, he would certainly not be averse to swap stamps. Paul should try it there. Does he, Paul, also collect foreign stamps? He, Edi, only collected Swiss stamps and would like to have all the Pro Juventute and Pro Patria stamp series.

After Paul O. has left, Edwin F. looks through the pile of letters and arranges them according to recipients, to whom he will then immediately deliver the letters intended for them. Most of the letters are for the doctors at the clinic and also for their families, who live on the clinic grounds. A few are for the clinic's administration. A few others for employees of the clinic, who live on the premises. A few letters for the patients of the clinic. Edwin F. pauses. A postcard, written in awkward script, is addressed 'To the esteemed office clerk, Edwin F.'. Edwin F. immediately recognizes his mother's handwriting. She writes, that his, Edi's, father, Ätti, has something important to discuss with him. He had to come home to Teufenthal for lunch on Sunday. There would be meat loaf, mashed potatoes and carrots for lunch.

Edwin F. sincerely hoped that there would be no heavy rains on Sunday. The weather must stay dry. He has no rain protection for cycling yet. He is lucky. The sun shines on Sunday. The ride takes two hours. He makes it to his parent's house in Teufenthal just before lunch. Ätti is surprised to see his eldest son suddenly standing in the living room. He does not know what urgent matters he should have to discuss with him. The mother, however, tells Edwin that she has a surprise for him. Beaming, she tells him, that there is a vacancy for an office clerk, an assistant to the municipal clerk, at the Municipal Office in Unterkulm. When she shyly had inquired, whether her Edi would have a chance of getting this job, the municipal clerk replied with great pleasure that ‚your Edi would be the ideal person for this job'.

"You're amazed, aren't you? Now you will finally have a decent job. For the 1st of November. What do you say now!", his mother ads and smiles at him expectantly.

Edwin F. is exasperated. How can he make clear to his mother, that he is not in the least thinking of giving up his good job in the Administrastion of the Königsfelden Clinic? He avoids to mention at home his new girl friend, Olga. Olga works in a trust office in Brugg and still lives with her parents in Rupperswil. No ten horses will get him, Edwin F., away from Olga and Königsfelden.

"I see, a job at the Municipal Office in Unterkulm is not enough for our son. Boy, o boy, don't you see, that we worry for you! Come on, Ätti, say something too. That you're working in the Monastery, a loony bin! I'm ashamed to tell people, when they ask me, where our eldest son is working. In the Monastery, of all places! Every reasonable person avoids to approach the Monastery. Otherwise, he'll go crazy himself. Boy, can't you imagine, how we suffer, that you are working there! Don't tell me, that you are in the good position to be a Cantonal Employee by this job. The Cantonal Employee does not weigh the Monastery. What a disgrace! How can you do this to us, to Ätti and me? Right, Ätti? Say something for once, Ätti."

Edwin F. loves his work as an office clerk in the Administration of the Königsfelden Clinic. He gets along very well with the administrator, the chief accountant and the two secretaries. He likes his work as well as the staff and the whole organization of the clinic.

The huge park of the former Königsfelden Monastery, then the local hospital, since 1872 the Königsfelden Cantonal Psychiatric Clinic, is situated between the small town Brugg, with roots in medieval times, and the village Windisch,.is beautiful. The park is surrounded by high walls, with a big entrance gate and gatehouse. The walls are due to the function of the area as a psychiatric clinic. The park is closed for the public. On entering the park is to the left of the entrance avenue the modern administration building situated behind high trees,. At the end of the avenue is the beautifully planted roundel with the Roman fountain in the middle. Behind it is situated the imposing, neo-classical main building, built in 1872. Consisting of a central part with three stories and large side wings to both sides. Like a castle.

In the main part the reception with the switchboard and a small kiosk, the office and the antechamber of the chief doctor, the offices of the other doctors and the nursing staff, the laboratory, the pharmacy and several function rooms are located on the First floor. On the second floor is the large appartment of the chief doctor and his family. On the third floor are the clinic's ballroom and chapel. In the side wings are on all three floors the wards for the patients, to the left the woman's wards, to the right the men's wards. The sidewings have big private gardens in front, protected with a fence of high iron poles. In order that the patiens can't run away. There are about 600 patients in the clinic and a staff of approximately 200 employees. In the courtyard behind the middle part of main building, framed by the backsides of both sidewings, is the huge kitchen, with staff rooms above it on higher floors. Next to the kitchen is the laundry, followed by the saddlery, the locksmith's shop, the sewing shop and the machine house. Standing near the roundel in front of the middle part of the main building, a gravel street past the deer enclosure, the open-air bowling alley and the exposed foundation walls of the west gate of the Roman camp of Vindonissa, the centuries-old lime tree in front of the 16th-century Old Hospital, which houses patient wards and staff flats, leads to the Gothic monastery church with its magnificent stained-glass windows and the Agnes Chapel next to it. Behind the church the stables of the farm are situated in the park, next to the house, where the head farmhand and the other farmhands with families live. In the stable are many cows, some bulls and swines as well. Spread over the park are various more recently built patients' pavilions, the carpenter's workshop, the house of the dead. In between these buildings are vegetable, fruit and flower gardens, a duck pond, a philosophers' path and, almost hidden, the snake pond, in the middle of which is enthroned a stone sculpture of Neptune with a trident. The clinic consists of a village of it's ow, simpliy as many patients, all the medical and administration staff with their families and many of the employees live here. Everyone knows everyone.

Edwin F. loves to live and work here and having contact with all kinds of people, regardless of whether they are doctors, patients, nurses or craftsmen. Of course, in his free time he meets up with colleagues in Windisch at the Sonne Pub or the Kohlenhof Pub to play a card game of Jass and have a beer. Or they meet in Brugg, at the somewhat classier Füchslin Restaurant, which also has a bowling alley. He spends the weekends and sometimes his weekday evenings with his dear Olga.

Edwin F. answers his mother with vaguely mumbled "yes, yes, yes". Ätti blinks at him behind the mother's back and shrugs his shoulders. The mother packs him a ham sandwich as a farewell. "So you won't starve on your way back to the Monastery". Edwin F. is annoyed at the way his mother fattenes him up. She had already forced a third and a fourth piece of meat loaf on him, at lunch, with the remark, "Now I've prepared your favourite meal as a surprise for you, don't disappoint me now, please!" As she says goodbye, she says once more, "Don't disappoint Ätti and me. Office clerc at the Municipal Office is such a fantastic chance !".Again Edwin F. mumbles, "yes, yes, yes". Then he is glad to be back on his steel donkey and to leave Teufenthal.

One fine day in the mail received from Postman Paul O. for the clinic and to be distributed by Edwin F. to the specific addressees, there is an open postcard from

Brugg Railway Station, Bulky Goods Department, to Doctor Hans Günther B.. The postcard announces to the German, that a parcel from Germany has arrived in the Bulky Goods Department for him and is now to be collected. With this doctor, Edwin F.'s conversations had never gone beyond a ‚Here you go' and ‚Thanks'. Except once, on one of the first really balmy spring evenings in May. The administrator of the Königsfelden Clinic, Edwin F.'s superior, suggests taking advantage of this fine weather and going for a few skittles after work. On the antique open-air bowling alley in the park of Königsfelden. Between the deer enclosure and the old hospital with the centuries-old lime tree in front of it. When they arrive at the bowling alley, Senior Doctor M. and the doctor from Germany, Doctor B., are already bowling there. The administrator wants to give up their plan and to retreat. But Doctor M., a most open person, asks the administrator and Edwin F. to join them and offers to bowl together as a foursome.

"Okay with you, dear colleague?", Senior Doctor M. asks the German. The German nods. But when they are bowling, they are concentrated on pushing the balls. Hardly any words are spoken. Except for recognition for successful throws, where the skittles just tumble. Or expressing disappointment when no skittles or only a few skittles fall. Edwin F. sees and hears how Senior Doctor M., the superior, and the German, the subordinate, constantly tease each other, are relaxed and seem to be excellent buddies. Edwin F. does not dare to speak freely in this company. Even though good comments are on the tip of his tongue now and then. This had been the only time, Edwin F. had spent any length of time near the German doctor.

Edwin F. offers to accompany Doctor B. to the railway station with a ladder cart, as the package seems to be bulky. So that he would not have to carry the bulky parcel on his own back to the clinic. At first, Doctor B. refuses Edwin F.'s help. Then he seems to reflect and finally, somewhat embarrassed, accepts Edwin F.'s offer. He even says, "Thank you very much, Office Clerk F.. Really obliging of you. My parents in Breslau had already announced by letter, that they would send me my bicycle. I'm certain that Mottl and Vatel had my bicycle well-packed so that it wouldn't get damaged on the way. And it really is better, to unpack it here then at the railway station!"

In the Bulky Goods Department at the Brugg Railway Station an official hand Doctor B. a huge, badly damaged, bulky parcel. The official apologizes. Swiss Customs had provided a condition report, according to which Swiss Customs had received the parcel in this badly damaged condition from the German Customs Authorities. This condition report, signed and stamped, was written in duplicate. The duplicate was for the doctor as proof to the German Reichsbahn that the damage had occurred in Germany. He, the official here in Brugg, had found the responsible office of the Deutsche Reichsbahn for the doctor and had written down its address on a piece of paper for the doctor. Edwin F. overhears the doctor thanking the official effusively and stealthily, trying to give him a generous tip. The official refuses in a huff. Whereupon the doctor's head turns red, and he turns away.

Edwin F. stows the bulky and badly worn package, from which individual parts of a bicycle are sticking out, on the ladder cart. Doctor B. wants to help, but is clumsy.

He is in the way of Edwin F.. Then Edwin F. pulls the ladder cart to Königsfelden. The doctor tries several times to grab the drawbar of the ladder cart himself. He acts so stupidly, that Edwin F. can easily push him away. Edwin F. can hardly recover from the sight of this package. He simply cannot imagine, how a simple parcel gets damaged in such a way on a simple rail transport. There must be something fishy about this transport. He sees from Doctor B.'s expression, that he does not want to get into any discussions about it. When they arrive in the clinic, Doctor B. does not bother to tell Edwin F. where the parcel is to be unloaded. Edwin F. heads for a bicycle stand in the Kitchen Yard. Doctor B. lets it happen. He lets Edwin F. peel the battered bicycle out of the package, which is badly torn in most places. Edwin F. stows the boxes and the wrapping paper on the ladder cart and presses the vehicle, which can hardly be called a bicycle any more, into Doctor B.'s hands. Earlier, Edwin F. happened to watch, how Doctor B. stealthily scratched the address label with the sender's address off the wrapping paper and put it in his jacket pocket. Edwin F. ssuspects, that this incidental behaviour together with Doctor B.'s aloofness, might be a clue to a secret.

"Well, Doctor, here we are. It is done," Edwin F. throws in.

"Thank you very much, Office Clerk F.. I guess I can throw this bicycle away."

"What an idea, Doctor! It can be repaired."

And the noble Doctor B. already disappeared. Not without first giving Edwin F. a nice tip. Edwin F. does not refuse it. He wonders if this conceited doctor will ever come down from his high horse.

Edwin F. tells his Olga about the experience with the German doctor and his bicycle.

"I be careful, not to offer that conceited German doctor my help ever again!"

"It had been a mistake to help him. Edi, Edi, just be careful that you don't get dragged into fishy things. You are simply far too naive and too good-natured. But you have to be very careful with Germans. Nowadays, it's not good to be too close to them. Let him deal with his own things. You know, when your superiors find out, that you're too close with this German..."

Olga once again manages to put into clear words the thoughts that are floating around diffusely in Edwin F.'s head. He marvels at her gift for always keeping things in perspective. If this doctor is already so distant towards him, Edwin F., he may also behave in a distant manner towards him, this doctor, without a guilty conscience. One should, Edwin F. thinks, be able to take such things lightly. But somehow ... He shoos away these irritating thoughts. He does not succeed. Somehow he makes fun of an impractical person, who is totally overwhelmed by the requirements of ordinary everyday life. German or not German doesn't matter. He certainly doesn't even know, how to put a jumped out bicycle chain back in again.

Edwin F. can't resist approaching Doctor B. occasionally and slyly asking, whether he has now got his bicycle repaired.

"Oh, Office Clerk F., I wanted to ask you for some time already, where there is a trustworthy and good bicycle dealer in the village."

"You don't want to throw away the damaged bicycle and buy a new one, Doctor! The frame of the bike is very good and undamaged. The front wheel too. The same goes for the handlebars. The chain is broken. But all the parts are still there. So, no problem. And the wobbly rear wheel can be fixed in no time at all ..."

Doctor B. cuts an insanely funny figure in Edwin F.'s eyes, as he stands in the landscape like a walking question mark. Edwin F. immediately takes the lead and shows the way. Astonished like a child, Doctor B. follows blindly all the instructions of Edwin F., the little office clerk. First Doctor B. fetches his broken bicycle from where he must have hidden it. Because he obviously is ashamed to call such a wreck his own. Then he follows Edwin F. with the thing to the ‚Maschinenhaus' (the wrought and locksmith workshop of the clinic) behind the Kitchen Yard. There Edwin F. explains to the head of the workshop, what they were up to, and asks for a place at a workbench, tools and cleaning threads. Then he starts to fiddle with the broken chain. He releases it from its wedging with the cogwheels and the frame. He begs one of the locksmiths to please mend the chain of Doctor B.'s bicycle. Edwin F. then unscrews the bent wheel from its fastening, clamps it in a vice and begins to gently pound with a wooden hammer. Doctor B. stands by the side and watches with his eyes wide open. Even his mouth stays wide open in amazement.

"My dear F., I am amazed. What a skilled man you are, unbelievable!"

"Oh, Doctor, it's not magic. Although an office clerk by profession, my passion is craftsmanship."

Edwin F. and Doctor B. look into each other's eyes. They both grin.

"I'm a loser when it comes to handicrafts."

Edwin F. swallows the remark on the tip of his tongue, that he had noticed this long ago.

After work, in beautiful weather, Edwin F. and Doctor B. pedal up through the Habsburg Mountain and Forest to what of the proud Habsburg Castle is left. Doctor B. almost runs out of breath on the way uphill. He is amazed at how easily Edwin F. manages the climb. Edwin F. consoles him that he, Doctor B., will soon have practice again. In the garden restaurant on the Habsburg, the Doctor B. treats Edwin F. to a few glasses of beer. He learns from Edwin F. that the beer here is ordered in vernacular as a ‚Stange hell' or ‚Stange dunkel' (light or dark rod). After a few rods, Doctor B. suggests to Edwin F. that they become more familiar with each other, as is customary here, unlike in Germany. Edwin F. can hardly believe that a doctor is offering him, an office clerk, to be on the more familiar first-name basis. At the same time, however, a horror runs through his limbs at the idea of how his dear Olga will react to this development of things. "Let's be on familiar terms! I'm Edi," Edwin F. throws out cheerfully and from then on addresses the Doctor B. as Hans Günther.

Olga once again reacts in a surprising way.

"Edi, Edi, you really are most astonishing. You are absolutely right. If someone is suspicious, you shouldn't keep your distance from him, but behave normally in a relaxed way. But if he then betrays himself, then you have to act. If he is secretly recruiting for the Nazis, if he is a spy, report it immediately to the authorities in Aarau and Bern. That's what I love about you, Edi. One thinks you are a nice boy and then one suddenly realizes, you are such a clever fellow."

Edwin F. wants to return the favour for the many beers at the Habsburg. He asks Hans Günther if he might invite him to the Kohlenhof Restaurant for a glass of Veltliner wine. Hans Günther is enthusiastic. Mentiones however, that he already knows the Kohlenhof and would be delighted to get to know a different place. While walking in the village Windisch, the Sonne Pub with the beautiful very ancient inn sign had caught his sight. It must be a traditional Swiss pub. Edwin F. winces in amusement. Laughingly he throws out, that the Sonne Pub is his favourite pub. A rustic pub. But much too simple for a doctor like Hans Günther. The simple villagers frequented the Sonne Pub.

"Edi, that's exactly where I want to go!"

Edwin F. is a bit scared to show up in the Sonne Pub, where all his buddies are, with a German in tow. Even if the German is a doctor, or precisely because he is also a doctor.

As was to be expected, his buddies greet Edwin F. with a big hello. Edwin F. waves furtively at them and tries to push Hans Günther to the back of the pub so that they can drink some glasses of Veltliner wine in peace. But his buddies won't leave him alone and desperately want him to sit down with them, introduce the foreigner to them and not to be strangers. One of the pals whispers to Edwin F., "Where did you pick this one up, and a German at that?"

When Edwin F. introduces Hans Günther as Doctor B. from Königsfelden, his buddies can hardly believe it. But Hans Günther is immediately interested in the card game they are busy with. He is taught that they were playing a card game called 'Jass'. In no time, Hans Günther is accepted into the merry circle. First he watches the others play a few rounds of Jass. Then he too is invited to join in. He is not very skilful, but manages to be accepted as a lousy player. Everyone is mighty proud to teach this German doctor from the Monastery, whom they are allowed to address as Hans Günther. Moreover, Edwin F. is envied for having such a fine gentleman as a friend.

On bycicle tours together, when they stop at a pub and have a bite to eat, Edwin enjoys the conversations with Hans Günther. Hans Günther is so clever, knows so much, has been around the world and knows it well. But when Hans Günther says that his greatest goal is to start a family and have a son, Edwin shakes his head. There is still time for all that. He wants to enjoy life a little more and hopes that his Olga will not start talking about engagement and marriage right away. There is still time for that. "We are still young. You too, Hans Günther. We are the same age, aren't we?"

Edwin doesn't quite understand why Hans Günther, as a doctor with a good job, doesn't marry his Hedy or someone else from his harem, if he is already so keen on marriage. Although, Edwin secretly thinks, Hans Günther probably cares more about a son, as he always says, than about the marriage itself. Whether Hans Günther, following Luther's recipe, has already planted a tree and now it is actually his turn to father a son in order to stand out as a real man?

Then again, when Hans Günther and Edwin meet to go on a pilgrimage together to the village, Hans Günther is totally dejected, whistles, as Edwin perceives with the greatest concern, from the last hole and whispers in a tearful voice, "The cow-Swiss don't love me. Now they are throwing me out of their little country for good!"

"Nonsense!" Edwin continues, "We have the forms at the administration for the extension of your work permit ..."

Edwin doesn't get any further with his speech because he notices how Hans Günther, the rascal, grins. This person, Edwin thinks, always manages to play something highly dramatic on me. I fall for it. And then it turns out that everything is only half as bad or not bad at all.

"Now, I almost fell for your act and really thought you were in trouble ..."

"If you lose your sense of humour, this endless paperwork becomes exhausting!"

Edwin is on his guard and from then on tries to catch on right at the beginning, when Hans Günther is trying to trick him again. Over time, he gets to know him better and can better assess Hans Günther's exaggerations. It's only Hans Günther's theatrics about his doctoral dissertation, that Edwin can't judge. That is beyond his horizon. When Hans Günther heartbreakingly whines that the professor in Bern is letting him down, is deliberately dawdling. Unfortunately, Edwin drops something about this matter to Olga.

"Then your Hans Günther is not a doctor at all?"

"You see, that's so, somehow he must be a doctor. After all, he works in the Monastery as a doctor. You wouldn't call him ..."

"It seems to me that it's another one of those little deals. But it is none of our business. One doesn't need to know everything"

Then Hans Günther whines again in the highest tones that doctor colleague P., the lucky devil, has been able to marry and will soon be a father, while he, the poorest Hans Günther, is condemned to remain a 'Hagestolz' (oldfashioned German word for eternal bachelor) all his life and to be abandoned by everyone. This time Edwin plays dumb and asks, "What is a Hagestolz?", and then adds, "If you don't mess around with Doctor P. so often any more because he has to look after his family, then we can have more beers and card games together!"

"Until you, Edi, let me down too," Hans Günther continues to lament, until he starts laughing again. Edwin can only shake his head at Hans Günther's chatter. He wonders why Hans Günther has to wage everywhere these shadow fights. As if, despite his short height and pale complexion, with his snappy demeanour and appearance, he is not man enough to stand his ground. How should I feel about my own situation? While Hans Günther is a doctor and respected by anybody, Hans Günther's prospects are, after all so much better then mine. His relationship with Hans Günther keeps him busy with such and similar considerations.

Olga does not let go. She understands that her Edwin has found a casual buddy in the German doctor for playing cards and riding his bicycle, but she still distrusts the peace. She wonders whether the all too naive and good Edi is not bringing himself into disrepute by his dealings with a German, of all people. Edwin is aware, that the other doctors at the clinic have also noticed how he, as a simple office clerk, keeps company with one of their own, a doctor, and a German at that.

Edwin knows that Senior Doctor M. is Hans Günther's direct superior. Senior Doctor M. is very approachable, never puts on airs in his position and is always open to the concerns of all the clinic's employees and patients. When one asks or tells him something, he always listens with interest and even asks questions. Edwin asks Senior Doctor M., if he thinks it is okay, that he occasionally plays cards or goes on bycicle rides with Doctor B.. Doctor M. laughs. That were not only okay. It were even a great benefit for both sides. Colleague B. gets to know Swiss everyday life and people from the village can reduce their reservations about Germans. Colleague B. did not have it easy. So, this distraction was most welcomed. Edwin does not dare to ask Senior Doctor M., in what respect Doctor B. had a difficult time. He also does not want to ask Hans Günther this question directly, as long as he does not begin to talk about real difficulties himself. From his round of Jass, he asks Guschti M., a well-respected local councillor in the village and, so to speak, the grey eminence of the Free Democrats, about his dealings with Hans Günther, the German doctor. He asks him directly whether he was making himself suspicious in the eyes of the village authorities by his dealings with a German.

"Typical you, F., you are such an honest skin. Don't worry about it. The authorities keep their eyes open and have not noticed any signs in Hans Günther, this Doctor

B., that he is politically active in any way. Do you think I would play a round of Jass with this German, if there was the slightest suspicion in him, that he were acting for the Nazis?"

Edwin is now so familiar with Hans Günther that he can ask him the question that is burning on his tongue, albeit in a roundabout way. The question about all the extraordinarily frequent private correspondence with Germany. But not only with Germany. With the whole world, too. Edwin thinks that for an average person, the correspondence is kept within bounds, a letter now and then, or a card to congratulate someone on a holiday. He has a guilty conscience because he overhears something, this extraordinarily large number of letters from abroad, which he might have to report to the authorities in today's dicey political situation, where the enemy can suddenly be in our midst. He takes the question asked some time ago by Postman Paul O. about possible swapping of stamps as a pretext to raise the subject and then skilfully let his genuine questions flow in spontaneously without any fuss. Hans Günther is happy to meet the postman, as he calls him, personally and to give him the exotic stamps he has in duplicate, if necessary to exchange them for Swiss stamps.

"As you know, I regularly make the pilgrimage to the meetings of the Stamp Association in Baden."

"I'm amazed at the huge number of letters you always receive from all over the world. How do you even get to write letters on top of your work? I gnaw on my pencil for hours when I'm supposed to write something, and then I've only written one sentence at the end, the letter is far from finished. I always hope that I can get on with it the next day.

"You see, Edi, that's the difference between us. You can do everything with your hands, and I'm always amazed at what a person can repair and produce! I am a prevented writer. My parents are retired, have nothing else to do, but write to me. They bombard me with letters and ask all my uncles and aunts to write to me often and as often as possible, under the pretext that I feel so abandoned in a foreign country. I cannot put an end to this avalanche of letters. How could I? Then we have countless adventurers in the relatives, who wanted to discover the farthest corners of the earth for themselves. And they are desperate to keep me informed about how well they are doing there. To persuade me to also emigrate to where they have a happy foothold."

"Yes, yes, in the last century, when there were famines here, people emigrated from here to America, South America and even Australia," Edwin acknowledges Hans Günther's explanations, which seem quite credible to him. He is sure that Hans Günther answered honestly. His answer had come as if shot from a cannon. Without the slightest hesitation. Edwin is reassured. He envies Hans Günther for his cosmopolitanism. Which he lacks, with his entire family living in Aargau. Only a great uncle had emigrated to America. Decades ago. But he was never heard from again.

Edwin doesn't hide from Olga when he occasionally goes out with Hans Günther to play cards or goes on a bicycle tour. Even when the weather is fine and the temperatures warm, he takes him on a bycicle ride over lunch to the lido in Brugg on the River Aare, where a group of clinic employees, including doctors, senior physicians, rarely even Chief K. himself, and now and then also the fine Miss K., the laboratory assistant from Königsfelden and at the same time the sister of the wife of Senior Doctor M., get together. Olga does not bring up the subject of Hans Günther again of her own accord. Which is fine with Edwin. However, he senses that the subject is still not completely off the table for Olga and that she still is suspicious.

A circumstance comes in handy. Hans Günther tells Edwin that Miss Sch., the house officer, has stood up for him and ensured that Chief K. has allocated him a new, larger room behind the Men C. ward. Now he wanted to show his appreciation to her, to thank her somehow. Should he invite her to dinner at the Du Parc Restaurant in nearby Baden? Edwin waves it off. Such a noble invitation could be misinterpreted. Marie, i.e. the house officer Miss Sch., was engaged. He and Olga knew her from the Wynenthal, the region where they all come from. Marie should not be talked about. Edwin has an idea, of which he passes on a small fragment to Hans Günther. Marie, as a house officer, eats together with the doctors in the doctors' dining room of the clinic. Hans Günther should ask Marie on Thursday after dinner, in front of all the other doctors, if he could invite her to a glass of wine at the Restaurant Füchslin to thank her for helping him change his private room in the clinic. If everyone knew what it was about, it would no longer be compromising for Marie. And the Füchslin, as Hans Günther knows, is a good middle-class restaurant, but not an upscale one.

"Without you, Edi, I would put my foot in my mouth one after the other. How would I survive without you here!"

Edwin knows he has a date with Olga on Thursday after dinner. He will suggest that they go to the Füchslin Restaurant for a glass of wine and see if there happens to be someone there, with whom they can have a drink and perhaps even play cards. Olga is always happy when Edwin suggests not the somewhat vulgar Sonne Pub, but the better Restaurant Füchslin. Olga doubts that they will find a suitable round for Jass at the Füchslin. Besides, the Veltliner wine is cheaper at the Kohlenhof. Edwin insists that they try Füchslin. If they don't find anyone there, they can always leave without a drink and head for the Kohlenhof. As soon as they enter the Füchslin Restaurant, Edwin notices at first glance that Marie is sitting with Hans Günther at a pretty table for four by a window, enjoying wine. He says nothing. Olga looks around carefully in search of a table that suits her. She drops, "There's no table left at the window ... Marie is sitting there with ... a stranger. Come on, Edi, don't act so embarrassed. We'll ask, if there's still room at their table and who knows, maybe we'll have the perfect round of Jass together there."

Olga is amazed when the stranger turns out to be the German Doctor B., Hans Günther. In no time at all a good conversation ensues. They agree to play a game of Jass. On the way home, Olga confesses to Edwin that this German is quite decent and also highly educated. He's got a lot going for him. And if even Marie keeps company with him, then he is beyond all doubt. After all, Marie could not afford anything improper. Her father was a colonel in the Swiss army. And in the general staff at that.

3.

Senior Doctor M. reads the police report from the files of patient P. and is surprised at what he discerns as the tendentious view of the reporting police officer. Instead of soberly recording observed facts, he lets qualifying expressions flow into the text, which are the outflow of a biased view. The next time he has contact with the Cantonal Police Department chief, he will casually mention to him, that it might be useful to train the police officers in reporting. Of course, he will talk to Chief K. – this is how the chief doctor of the Königsfelden Clinic ist called by all of his staff – about it beforehand. In order not to expose himself again to the accusation of unauthorized forward bouncing. Chief K. has proved to be sensitive about the clinicians' contacts with State Authorities in Aarau and Bern.

A somewhat hesitant and delicate knock on his office door startles Senior Doctor M. out of his thoughts. He hates to be disturbed while thinking. Disturbances scare away good thoughts, that then are lost forever. This rather gentle knocking on his office door makes him sit up straight in his office chair behind his desk. Knockings generally are fierce. He has no idea who might be at the door.

"Come in!"

Senior Doctor M. stifles a grin as he sees Bertie, his wife, poke her head through the door, which is open a crack. He didn't expect her in the least. Bertie avoids whenever possible disturbing him during work in his office.

"Sorry, Peter. I know I shouldn't disturb you in your work. It's urgent. And a delicate matter. It cannot wait until lunch. I've left little Peiderlein with Gloria in Chef K's antechamber for a moment, where he can sit at an unused writing desk."

"Come on in! Why on earth are you withholding my son from me? After all, Peider is already one and a half years old and can trudge into my office on his own little legs."

"Peiderlein is always happy when he is allowed to be with Gloria. Besides, he shouldn't hear anything that he can't yet understand, and that isn't for him. Just now, I received a telephone call at home. Porter D. operates the switchboard today. He announced a telephone call from Germany. To me. At home. When he said that he would now connect, I interrupted him and said that it was probably a misunderstanding. He should connect with you. He then said that the lady, whose name he did not catch, had specifically asked for Mrs. Senior Doctor Bertie Mohr. The lady turned out to be Doctor B.'s sister, who lives in Hirschberg, Silesia. A very friendly and fine lady, as I could gather from the few words we exchanged. She told me the sad news, that B.'s father, Vatel, had died of a heart attack in Breslau. Mottl, the mother, had immediately written a letter to B. and taken it to the post office. Vatel's death, however, must be a terrible blow for B.. She did not want her brother to hear this news alone in a quiet room while reading Mottl's letter. B. had mentioned several times in his letters how understanding and friendly Senior Doctor M. and his wife behaved towards him. She now asked me, Bertie, to break the sad news to her brother gently, so that he would be prepared for Mottl's letter. I did not know what to reply. Of course, I told the nice lady that we would fulfil her wish. - I possibly can't give this terrible message to B., Peter. I know him too little for that. It must be a talk among men. Besides, you know B. much better than I do. After all, you are his superior. It probably doesn't make sense to let Gret in on it first. I know my little sister. She is quickly overwhelmed in difficult situations. Besides, she doesn't know B. that well. Just because she is a lab technician and has to deal with doctors in the clinic professionally. Or accompanies B., if he can't find any other company, to the lido or the cinema ..."

"Or goes dancing with him at the Kursaal in Baden!"

"It doesn't matter. You, you must break the terrible news to B., and gently. You know how to talk to people so well. Even when it gets totally difficult. You have such a calming way."

Peter smiles. His dear Bertie beats around the bush for a long time until she finally gets to the point. Peter realizes after the first few words, that he is now being challenged. He lets Bertie finish. Until she runs out of words. She huffs, stepping impatiently from one foot to the other, "I can rely on you, Peter. So, now I have to pick up Peiderli at Gloria's, otherwise he'll turn her entire office upside down. And as Chief K.'s secretary, she certainly has better things to do than look after little children".

Peter must talk to Colleague B. at once. Without further delay. It is important, that Colleague B. gets the news, before Porter D., who knows about the phone call from Germany spreads the news in the whole clinic, that a woman from Germany, from enemy territory, has called and and asked to speak to Mrs. M.. Such a rumor musn't, by chance, reach Colleague B. and worry him, before he knows from him, Peter, what has happened.

Peter must go to B.'s office immediately. B. shares his office with colleague P.. P. does not need to hear what Peter has to tell B.. Although P. and B., as Peter has observed with satisfaction, have become close friends and do many things together. Even after P. got married about a year ago, later became a father and is allowed to live outside Königsfelden in the village of Windisch with his small family and with a special permit from Chief K. and the Cantonal Health Department in Aarau.

Peter calls Colleague B. by phone. Fortunately, he is at his workplace. Peter asks him to come to his office immediately. Peter himself is startled by his accidentally escaped command tone. He fears, that the conscientious B. will rack his brains as to what he might have done wrong at work, that his senior doctor is ordering him around like this. Peter throws down in a relaxed tone, "Don't worry, dear colleague, you won't be beheaded." Even for this lazy remark, Peter thinks, it is, in this situation, inappropriate and out of line. Poor guy, B., Peter thinks spontaneously. And : How do I tell my child?! While in his imagination, B. and his relationship with him come to life in his memory in a split second.

One fine day, more than two years ago, Chief K. announces, that he had succeeded in filling the vacant assistant doctor position. The entire staff breathed a sigh of relief. When Chief K. let slip, as if in passing, that the new employee and colleague was German, most of them pulled long faces.

At that time, before the war had been directly immanent and then had begun not quite a year ago, Peter had thought, it was courageous of Chief K. to show openness and hire a young German. Whereas Chief K., as the head doctor of a cantonal clinic, is otherwise always careful to maintain good relations with the Cantonal Health Department in Aarau. To avoid stirring up a hornet's nest. Where in the highest cantonal circles in Aarau a subliminal battle between anti-German and pro-German is smouldering. With his decision to employ a young German as an assistant doctor and to obtain a work permit for him, Chief K. provokes one side or the other.

Peter is eagerly awaiting to having a young German colleague. Since his semester at the universitiy in Berlin, he admires the Germans and their way of openly addressing everything and not shying away from contradictions. What he loves about the Germans is precisely what annoys many conservative Swiss, as they don't feel up to this openness. To Peter's great surprise, Chief K. makes a castling among the doctors by shifting the senior doctors and the assistant doctor here and there between the different patients wards, so that the new one, the German, became subordinate to him, Peter, in the Men A to C ward.

The German has Prussian dash, is worldly, well-educated and jovial. Peter is convinced that he will turn out to be a competent colleague. Peter also notices with satisfaction that B. is open and friendly to everyone, so that he is soon not only the darling of the fair ladies, but also a welcome colleague among the assistant doctors and the entire staff of the clinic. The original prejudices of almost everyone are blown away. B. tells Peter many interesting things about Berlin, Breslau, Halle, Heidelberg. In no time at all, they have a stimulating exchange about non-professional topics, such as literature, film and theatre, which interests them both. As if by magic, Peter and B. develop not only professional, but also personal and stimulating relations.

Peter lives with his family in a pretty single-family house in the clinic area, behind the Old Hospital and the Gothic Monastery Church and near the duck pond, the vegetable garden and the stables of the farm. It is their custom, to drink every day after lunch a mocha, which they call our black coffee. Peter soon asks B. to join him and his wife for their black coffee, after his, B.'s, lunch in the doctors' dining room of the clinic.

"My wife is happy to meet you. You and we live so close to each other. She has already heard about you. After lunch, we always listen to the news on the radio at half past one and then have our black coffee around one o'clock. We expect you just before one o'clock. Then we have a good hour to chat a bit before the two of us get back to our work at two o'clock."

Bertie is blown away by Doctor B.. Admires him for his education. His worldliness. His elegant appearance and for his knowledge of literature. She is amazed to discover, that he also reads his Homer in the original language, Ancient Greek. The two agree to read a few pages of Homer together over a glass of wine from time to time in the evening. Peter, in turn, discovers that B. plays chess. Now and then they play a game of chess in the evening, also over a glass of wine. It comes in handy for Peter that B.'s desire to play chess is stronger than his ability.

Consequently, they play playfully without any particular pressure to win. Sometimes, when other visitors show up, there is an opportunity for a game of Jass. Gret, Bertie's youngest sister, is often the fourth in the group. She works as a laboratory assistant in the clinic. Coincidentally, she had started her job in the Königsfelden Clinic on the same day as B.. She keeps a cool head towards Doctor B.. She can stand up to him, which also seems to amuse him. Then Peter drags B. to his bowling round at the Füchslin Restaurant. In no time at all a casual social contact develops which, as Peter notes with satisfaction, Also B. enjoys and which seems to make the foreigner more familiar to him. B. settles in well in his new environment at Königsfelden and seems to feel at home here. He is totally infatuated with Peter and Bertie's little son, Peider. He spoils the little one with presents. The little one enjoys it.

"It must be a dream to have such a strapping offspring, a son and heir," B. says in rapture. Peter listens. It seems to him that B., who is still young and has the world and life open to him, really envies his family situation.

"Especially when the child absolutely refuses to obey and stamps the floor in defiance," Peter adds with a grin.

Peter notices that B. has the reputation of being a womanizer. He studiously conceals this fact from Bertie. Although, at the same time, B. seems to be dreaming of an idyllic family and a son and heir. He turns the heads of many a female being. And they like to have their heads turned by him. Fortunately, Peter thinks, Gret is immune to sentimentalities and doesn't let herself be particularly impressed by a Don Juan. Besides, when she is with him, Doctor P., Office Clerk F. or other staff members of the clinic are usually with them as well.

Thus, B. actually turns out to be an ideal colleague and likeable guy for Peter, with whom serious conversations and light-hearted partying are possible in addition to the professional dealings. Soon after they had started to work together, B. had confided in Peter under the seal of secrecy, that psychiatry was not at all his desired field of medicine. He had been pushed into it by his father, Vatel, and Professor Strassmann in Berlin. Therefore, he did not know whether he was up to the task. Subsequently, however, he proves to be an explorer of the human psyche with flair, is willing to learn and interested. And he apparently likes to have psychiatric reports imposed on him. Ordered by penal authorities and law courts. His assistant doctor colleagues like to avoid this task. With a grin, B. likes to joke, as he has failed in making a living with his writing, that he at his regular work as a doctor may now write up stories as a substitute. As a poet, he already had several publications. The writing of psychiatric reports therefore suited him perfectly. B.'s reports are perfectly researched and written. Peter soon considers him indispensable for the clinic, not only because of his work as an expert for reports. Which is also a perfect argument when it comes to extending colleague B.'s work permit with the Migration Departments in Aarau and Bern. Peter is able to briefly greet B.'s parents, Vatel and Mottl, on the occasion of their holiday in Switzerland, when they visit B. in the Königsfelden Clinic and also have a conversation with Chief K.. Peter's brief glance at B.'s old man together with B. confirms to him that the father still has his son in full control. Chief K. is totally blown away by B.'s parents. "Such differentiated, interested, really fine gentlemen. It was a great pleasure to show B.'s father around the clinic. The highly decorated officer in the Great War and medical councillor, Sanitätsrat Doctor. B. and his charming wife."

For some time now, Chief K. has been thinking of publishing a periodical. For a better cohesion of the many-headed clinic staff and for a selected public as a reference for the clinic, which is too little known and accepted outside its surrounding walls. In B., Chief K. finds the right editor for the new peridocal. Doctor B. suggests as name of the peridocal ‚Herbstgruss' (Autumn Greetings). Peter knows that this assignment is not a self-evident sign of trust from Chief K. towards the young assistant doctor. B. fulfils the task with flying colours. The 'Autumn Greetings' are published once a year with a mixture of information from the clinic, background articles and also contributions by patients and staff.

The political world situation is deteriorating. Disturbing news from Germany reaches Switzerland. War breaks out at Germany's instigation. Peter is surprised how B., who as a German is doubly affected by the political developments, seems to shrug it all off without batting an eyelid. He never says a word about whether he will be drafted into the Wehrmacht and if not, why not. In response to questions, B. assures Peter, that he does not have to do military service in Germany. He does not explain why he is so sure of it. He continues to work as usual with great commitment. But he has to do a lot of extra work. The Swiss colleagues, including Peter, are called up to the military in turn and for shorter or longer periods of time. Additional work falls to B., who takes it on without a murmur. He proudly shows Peter, who is currently on home leave and temporarily working in the clinic again, a field postcard he has received from Office Clerk F., who has been called up for a longer period of time and, as B. adds, is now going to marry his Olga. Astonished that Fräulein K., Peter's sister-in-law, is a sergeant in the Women's Military Auxiliary Service, B. also shows Peter the field postcard he received from her.

Peter knows from his own experience what it means to have to look after oneself and to strugle in order to survive. His father, a priest and descendant of a noble Graubünden (the Grisons) family, but without a fortune, marries a daughter from the best and at the same time wealthy family. Before the Great War, he invests his wife's entire fortune in German papers, hoping for great profits. After the Great War, the papers are no longer worth anything and the money is gone. His father earns too little as a village pastor to be able to finance the studies of several sons. Peter has to and wants to come through his medical studies, with several jobs on the side, to earn his living and to be financially independent. Without parental support. His studies and the various jobs by the side sometimes bring him to the brink of exhaustion. He makes it. Without grumbling. He has experienced his actually difficult fate as a formative experience and is still somehow proud of the fact, that he has come through well despite everything and has achieved something. He is reluctant to talk about it. Knowing his own fate, he can vividly imagine that not everything goes smoothly for a German in Switzerland at the end of the 1930s or beginning of the 1940s. That he probably has to struggle with big difficulties. But B. keeps his mouth shut and fights his fights in the shadow at best.

In the most diverse discussions, B. never tires of emphasizing how he shares the concerns about the political world situation, but seems surprisingly uninvolved and distant to Peter. B. never expresses personal thoughts. Peter notices that he can talk easily with him about general topics. However he blocks it as soon as it becomes personal. Peter takes it calmly as his own idiosyncrasy. After all, he knows that he should not interfere in other people's lives in an unwanted way. B. is an independent thinker and will probably have his reasons for communicating the way he does. But then Peter happens to catch a glimpse of a postcard that B. has received from his parents in Breslau. He notices that next to his mother's first name, Elfriede, is the name Sarah, and next to his father's, Eugen, is the name Israel. The scales fall from Peter's eyes. B. is not in Switzerland voluntarily, as he would like to appear. He is a Jew. That is why he is not drafted into the military, even though he is German. B. describes himself as a Lutheran. As Peter knows, he attends services in the Protestant church in Windisch. He also takes part in a Bible study group there. Peter thinks, smart guy, the perfect cover. He brings up the topic in a conversation with Chief K.. Chief K. tells him that B. had confessed his situation to him, the head doctor, under the seal of secrecy. B.'s parents were born Jews and had only been baptized shortly after B.'s birth and before his baptism. B. was, in fact, a Lutheran. According to the German racial laws, he was nevertheless considered as a full Jew because of his ancestry. He, Senior Doctor M., should not make use of this knowledge. B. did not want it to be discussed. Peter is startled out of his musings about his past history with B. by another, this time a firm, knock on his office door.

Peter knows that B. will be standing in front of him in a moment. He must convey the sad news to him. Peter asks B. to take a seat at the small meeting table. He sits down opposite him. From the brief, startled look that Peter immediately catches on B's face, probably at the now unusual treatment, Peter assumes that he senses the extraordinary nature of the situation. B. immediately regains his composure after hearing the news. He listens to the sad news with apparent stoic calm. Then he says in a toneless voice, "Thank you, esteemed Colleague". And he prepares to get up and leave his senior doctor's office.

"My dear B., let me know if there is anything I can do for you. I feel for you. It is terrible to lose one's father. And even more so, as there is no way to say goodbye to him properly."

B. turns around once more. Shows his pain-distorted face.

"I can't stand by Mottl. The war. Germany. Me here in Switzerland. The poorest Mottl. Alone."

"At least your sister is with her. And she seems to be a most sensible lady."

"Yes. And the not so little Ilsetraut. 12 years old by now. And little Pimmer. Karl-Heinz, 6 years old. Mottl's grandchildren. Of whom Vatel had also been so incredibly proud. And my brother-in-law, a good guy. Who, as a banker, can advise Mottl."

Peter keeps a bottle of cognac and a few glasses in a cupboard in his office for special occasions. He asks B. to take a seat once more and offers him a cognac. Peter still can't shake the impression that he can't really get to him. That B. has probably only dropped the top mask of stoic calm, for a brief moment, and let his true face shine through, or perhaps it is just another mask. At least B. opens up to Peter to the extent, that he confesses to him, how he infinitely admires his father, the widely respected doctor and highly decorated officer in the Great War, and cannot imagine never seeing him again. The Nazi regime must have affected him so much. Vatel's heart surely could not have kept up with all the humiliations, insults and torments. Peter observes with slight irritation, how B. keeps his composure even in the now intimate conversation and does not even talk about his own feelings, his current state of mind, about his helplessness. The conversation remains an exchange of appropriate, thoroughly honest thoughts. Peter tries to imagine B.'s actual mental state. He fears that this thoroughly controlled person, who does not seem to let anyone get close to him, could implode. Peter dislikes to run after his Colleague B. in order to see his possible reactions right away. After all, it would be presumptuous to act like a nanny and make B. feel, that he cannot be trusted to look after himself and take responsibility for himself.

After the conversation with B., Peter has a brilliant idea. He pretends to be wandering, rather aimlessly, in the corridors of the clinic, but heads purposefully for the laboratory. He enters the lab, casually and slowly, as if he happened to be passing by, and it suddenly occured to him here, that he could stick his head inside the lab. He wants to ask his sister-in-law Gret, the laboratory assistant at the clinic, known in the clinic as Fräulein K. or Nurse Marga, with an innocent expression, how she is feeling today.

Peter and Gret get along splendidly. Not least because Peter, when he joined the K. Family, which totally fascinates him, managed to secretly observe the brilliantly ingrained patterns within the smaller and larger K. Family unit and, for the fun of studying the seemingly successful coexistence of an extended family, to question it analytically. He soon noticed Gret's special position in the family. Gret is the youngest of the three K. daughters. They are all of one heart and soul. They all like Gret's cheerful manner. But something, Peter senses, is wrong. Bertie thinks, he is seeing ghosts. He cannot and will not ask Nänne and Vatter, his so good and dear parents-in-law. Peter can't understand why everyone seems to be genuinely worried about this vivacious and enterprising young woman Gret.

On a Sunday family walk in Oberrohrdorf, where the parents-in-law live and own a stately home, the whole family, together with random guests who happen to be visiting the K. Home, which is known far and wide, first goes to the Gallows Hill, then to the family vineyards and to their own forest. Peter manages to stay a little behind, together with Gret. He asks her, when they are among themselves, why the whole family seems to worry about her. Gret laughs brightly.

"That's a long story. I don't want to bore you with it. Well, now that you mention it ... Well, I was a nanny and governess in Paris for a year, just like Bertie before me, with the Meyer family, then - also to learn Italian - with a family in Florence. The husband was a general by Mussolini's grace. The wife, a constant migraine-advancing beauty. The little son was a lively little fellow, whom I took care of with the greatest joy. The wife often fled to the country house because of her migraine and left us in the city. Somehow, a rumour got around, that also reached my parents in faraway Oberrohrdorf. I were having an affair with the general. Or at least with the general's chauffeur. Well, you know Vatter, my father. He's just the way he is. I received a telegram in Florence. 'Nänne seriously ill stop come back immediately stop if you still want to see her alive'. You can imagine how excited I was. Nänne, my mother, this soul of a human being ... I rush home head over heels. At home, Nänne is chirpy. Since then, I have been the problem child. The one you have to keep from going astray."

"And, with whom did you have the affair, with the general or the chauffeur," Peter asks curiously without thinking much.

Gret laughs and doesn't answer.

To find out how badly Gret is hurt by Vatter's behaviour, Peter sighs, "It must be terrible for you to have been betrayed like that by your own father."

Again Gret laughs. Theoretically, it were certainly true. But she adds, that Vatter is just the way he is. And she likes him very much. Although it is not always easy to get along with him and his stubborn K. head. Of course, immediately after her return from Florence and when she was no longer allowed to go back to Florence, she thought the world would collapse. Soon, however, she realized how amusing the fact had been, that the clever Vatter had been able to catch her and pull her over the coals. All the anger, annoyance and pain vanished. After all, she did not have to decide herself in the matter. It had been decided for her. Possibly, the best solution for her. The fact that she is now the declared problem child of the family gives her a pleasant leeway and freedom.

"You don't speak so openly with your sister and your parents," Peter asks.

"Certainly not! Then they would finally declare me crazy. That they are so worried about me, shows that they love me. Should I not have been quite so open with you? Are you going to get into trouble with Bertie?"

"It's all between us. Our little secret," Peter reassures Gret, who doesn't seem genuinely worried. Who walks beside him, grinning. Quickening her pace to catch up with the others again.

Since this confession, there has been a special understanding between Gret and Peter. Even Bertie sometimes jokingly throws in, "You shouldn't have married me, you should have married Gret. She, unlike me, takes nothing in life seriously."

The good understanding between Peter and Gret is strictly limited to intellectual exchange. Gret had been offered a room by Bertie and Peter in their family home on the clinic grounds when she took up her laboratory assistant position at the clinic, which Peter had arranged for her. She had preferred, like the clinic's normal employees, to be allocated a room between patient wards. So it is quite appropriate that every now and then, if Peter happens to be passing by the lab, he pokes his head in, looks to see if Gret is there, and if so, exchanges a few words with her.

"Hello, long time no see. How are you?", Peter asks Gret.

Peter sees that Gret is currently handling test tubes, liquids and Bunsen burners. He adds that he didn't want to disturb her. He himself were in a hurry.

"I'll drop any job for my favourite brother-in-law," Gret returns with a laugh, without taking her eyes off the liquid in the test tube

Peter quickly gets to the point. He urgently needed her help. He enlightens her about the death of B.'s father in Breslau, about his own inability to dig in his heels to make sure he doesn't implode.

"A catastrophe," Gret gasps, "B. is totally fixated on his father. - Now you want me to ...? All right. Are you seriously afraid he might hurt himself?"

"I don't know."

"I'll go to his office in a minute and ask him ... There's that new Zarah Leander film on at the cinema Odeon. I'll pretend, I don't know anything about his father's death. Then I can... Yes, yes, let me do it. - Not that you think I have it in for him ...", Gret adds in a strange tone.

The regular exchange about B.'s condition welds Peter and Gret into an even more conspiratorial community. If they meet by chance or plan to meet in a quiet place, where no one can hear them, Peter doesn't need to ask any questions. Gret blurts right out.

"Brother-in-law, my brother-in-law, you got me into this, that I have become Hans Günther's wailing wall ...", Gret complains in an exaggeratedly dramatic tone.

"You are on a first-name basis?"

"You don't seriously believe that I can elicit personal details from him without feigning a certain closeness. Besides, what's the big deal with young people being on a first-name basis. Please don't tell me that it's not proper for a little lab assistant to be on familiar terms with one of the gods in a white coat. After all, he is also on first-name terms with Edi F., the office clerk. And anyway, the fact that he doesn't act quite so arrogant as a German is amazing and ..."

"Seriously, Gret, if it's too much for you to watch over B., we can stop the exercise. It seems to me that he's quite composed ..."

"The wailing wall thing, well, the truth is, he never complains. We're not that intimate. Just buddies. Besides, it's not his style to talk about personal things. As you know yourself ... When, according to your assignment, I made it a point to intercept Hans Günther at every conceivable opportunity and to feel his pulse, he had deliberately eluded me. But then, as chance would have it, we met by chance in Baden. On the Theatre Square. In front of the 'Flieger' (Flyer), this monumental sculpture by Hans Trudel. He was standing in front of it, lost in thought, looking at this figure. I crept up and startled him with, 'Well, Doctor B. ...'. He quickly regained his composure. I asked him if he liked the sculpture? I told him that Nänne was friends with this sculptor and freak from Baden. That Bertie had a small sculpture of his. That led to a good conversation. He invited me to an ice cream coupe in the Himmel (heaven) Tea Room. Afterwards we watched the film 'Pépé le Moko' at the Cinema Royal - with Jean Gabin, a must-see! - and afterwards, at his suggestion, we went dancing at the Kursaal before catching the last train to Brugg. He suggested to me on this occasion that we become on a first-name basis. As he had learned from Edi, people in Switzerland are much less reticent about being on first-name terms than in Germany. And his 'complaints'. He never complains. He tells me disgusting stories, incidents from Germany, with cynical comments, pure satire. As if it's none of his business. Yet, I know very well that he or his relatives in Germany have experienced and are experiencing precisely these disgusting things. The man is a mystery to me. He doesn't let, what happens to him, get to him and lives his life happily, as it seems. I suspect that he wants to process what he has experienced in a novel. And he's using me as a guinea pig, so to speak, to find out whether the stories work. As far as facts are concerned, I learned from his stories that in Germany Christians whose ancestors were Jews, are also treated as Jews. I had not known that. That Jewish students - and also Christian students whose ancestors were Jews - are no longer allowed to study at universities and cannot find a professor who will accept them as doctoral students. That before the war, some time before the war, Jews - even Christians whose ancestors were Jews - had to hand in separate statements of their assets to the authorities. That then, after the Reichskristallnacht, the shameful reparation payments imposed on Jews also had to be paid by Christians whose ancestors were Jews. To the amount of one third of their assets. That Jews, even Christians whose ancestors were Jews, were no longer allowed to own gold or silver. That they had to hand over their precious metals to the authorities, except for two or three sets of silver cutlery in daily use. That on Aryans married to Jewish women, even Christian women whose ancestors are Jews, are pressured to separate from their wives. It took a while for the scales to fall from my eyes. Hans Günther must have experienced these things himself or in his immediate family environment. Peter, imagine! If all this is really his story! And he doesn't breathe a word about his own persecution. He must have experienced terrible things. He continues to experience it. Without making a face. Without batting an eyelid. Edi told me this story about Hans Günther's bike, which had arrived from Germany completely demolished. How Hans Günther hadn't lost his composure in the slightest. Now I realize that the ruffians of the Nazis deliberately smashed up the 'Jewish' property on the way, even though Hans Günther's parents, Vatel and Mottl, had

had to pay a lot of money for the export permit. Can you, you clever house, explain to me, how Hans Günther manages to let the terrible things roll off him, how they don't seem to touch him. So that he can go on living normally. I would be exhausted if I had to experience something like that. It's pure madness how, in the shadow of an apparently successful life, a struggle of life, fights for survival take place without us noticing anything."

Peter learns things about B. from Gret that don't really surprise him. He wonders how, in the everyday life of people with whom one is frequently and closely together for professional or social reasons, one unquestioningly takes the externality of the factual for granted. He shakes his head that it hadn't occurred to him to ask B. one question or another. But now Gret tells him how she dedicates herself with devotion to his, Peter's, mission and thus answers all the questions that are open in him, but which Peter was not aware of as such. He shakes his head in amazement at how fate plays with coincidences and listens with great interest to what Gret has to tell him.

For Peter, the two of them, Gret, who seems to have no interest in a new love affair, and B., who seems to respect that this woman is too good for a little love affair on the side, are the prime example that a good and valuable friendship between a man and a woman can indeed work.

Then it comes as it must. Not that Peter never thought of a possible love affair between Gret and B. or had the slightest objection to it. In the meantime, B. is also Hans Günther to him and Bertie. Peter is amazed at Gret, who doesn't seem to care a jot that not only in the wider environment of the clinic, among the people who have to deal with Hans Günther and her on a daily basis, heads are shaken about how a young woman from a good family gets involved in a flirtation with a foreigner, and a German, of all people, at that, and in these times. It is clear to Peter that this relationship suits Hans Günther. After Hans Günther envies the doctor's Colleague P. and Office Clerk F. so much for their marriage and soon-to-be fatherhood, it is clear that he is no longer out for flirtations, but for real love that has a future in the prospect of starting a family.

Even before the family had been made privy to Gret and Hans Günther's budding love, Peter is sitting on pins and needles because he keeps his knowledge of this love a secret even from his Bertie, lest something of it, even unintentionally, get through to Nänne and Vatter before its time, Gret bursts into Peter's office early one Monday morning in the beautiful month of July 1940. Her words almost spill over with joy and the urge to share, and her face beams.

"Just imagine, Peter, yesterday on our trip to the Montain Rigi - the weather was so beautiful and the view so wonderful - at the Rigi-Kaltbad Inn, when Hans Günther was eating an ice cream coupe and I a slice of Linzertorte (cake), he suddenly gets funny. At first, I'm startled. What a mood he has. He turns away. He avoids my gaze. And then begins to talk in a mumble. I think, oh dear, what has got into this man, I don't know him like that. He squeezes at words. Until I realize that he wants to explain his origins and his lack of prospects in life. And hence the impossibility of our relationship. He can't commit to a woman he takes seriously and loves in his shitty personal situation. He sits there like a heap of misery and shovels ice cream into his mouth as if mechanically. I am so impossible. Instead of showing compassion, I exploded in a laugh. I immediately apologized. Confessing to him, that I had already guessed his difficult personal siuation. If I didn't love him so much and didn't care at all about the fact, that he and his family were ostracized, I would never, ever have got involved with him. You should have seen how this man, just a moment ago a heap of misery, straightened up and beamed at my words ..."

"He is a really honest man," admits Peter. „He is not the show-off certain colleagues consider him to be. His demeanour must somehow be a protective armour that allows him to survive unmolested. Now is the time when you or I can let Bertie in on your love story, so that she, who can't keep anything to herself, can give Nänne and Vatter a heads-up ..."

Bertie says mockingly, "Typical, my little sister, who takes nothing in life seriously, catches this perfect gallant man - well, apart from the fact that he has to be German, of all people, but for a German .... I don't know anyone as educated and appealing and the best choice of man my little sister has ever hooked up with."

Nänne is smitten by Hans Günther. She goes into raptures.

"Such an educated person. Such good manners. So open and friendly. Well, it flatters a woman when someone is so gallant, not such a crude wooden peg. And he comes from the country of my favourite poet, Heine!", Nänne says about Hans Günther after his first visit, when Peter asks her, how she liked him. Peter is always amazed at his mother-in-law's spontaneous knowledge of human nature.

"But Peter, don't think you have to make conversation with us women out of politeness. All the other men except you are in the Leuen Inn. Yes, yes, even Doctor B.. Vatter dragged him along right away. Said, so that you, Doctor, can also get to know the common people here in the village. The Doctor followed him enthusiastically. Go now over to the Leuen Inn yourself, Peter, ..."

Peter is most irritated, when he hears several times from politically or socially important personalities, how they are gossiping that Vatter K., of all people, this prominent personality, both professionally and politically, this liberal, cosmopolitan and upright Swiss, has so little control over his youngest daughter, that she is fooling around with a German - just imagine: a German of all people! Peter warns Vatter, his opinionated and outspoken father-in-law with the stubborn K.-head, about what he has overheard. Vatter looks at Peter with big eyes. Peter spontaneously slips into the role of a little schoolboy. Vatter laughs out loud. As a grown man, one should not be impressed by such gossip. For him, the only thing that counts, is the human being. Doctor B. were an upright man. He understands the choice of his youngest daughter. Even if he is very disappointed that she, just like the two older ones, has found herself a doctor, when a veterinarian would be a real asset with all the animals in his stable.

Peter is amazed at how a relationship of trust is immediately established between his family-in-law and Hans Günther. Nänne and Vatter see Hans Günther as one of their own right from the start. Peter and Gret are totally amazed when Hans Günther tells them the story of Vatter's and Nänne's life, as they know it only rudimentarily. Without all the details that Vatter and Nänne had obviously now told Hans Günther. Peter confesses to Hans Günther, that he had experienced Vatter as not really communicative, but rather introvert.

"Oh, come on, Peter! Someone who is kind of the secret ruler in the national professional association and regionally in politics and to whom everyone listens cannot possibly be an introvert. As he's never told you anything about himself, it's just that you've never really got hold of him. I love your old folks. Take care of them. They're very special. From the fragments of Mr. and Mrs. K.'s tales, I could now easily and vividly write an exciting novel. - Your gnarled Vatter, as you both know, is not a man of big words. But when he says something and starts talking, often in a grumbling way, it has a lot of substance. Imagine how he, as a liberal politician, is a respected figure in the village, in the region and in the canton. As a cheese and milk merchant with cheese dairies in various regions of Switzerland and also a cheese dairy in French Savoy, he must be a shrewd businessman and entrepreneur. Vatter is a cunning storyteller. As the eldest son of a well-heeled milk and cheese merchant and farmer, he is left empty-handed when it comes to inheriting his parents' farm. As the youngest son inherits the farm. According to the peasant inheritance laws in the area. The reason of this law is, that the parents could still pay for an appropriate education for the older sons in any case. So Vatter, as the eldest son, was sent by his parents in 1886 to a posh boarding school in French speaking part of Switzerland to get the appropriate finishing touch, when he was 16 years old. In the company of the noble gentlemen's sons at the boarding school there, Vatter was ridiculed as a country bumpkin. Until he showed the noble lacquer monkeys the way things are. During a sunday walk he catapults the peer leader headfirst into the meadow border in a one-on-one fight. From then on, Vatter is respected. Nevertheless, he feels, that he is not in the right place in this boarding school. He figures out that it would be better for him to attend a commercial school in Neuchâtel. In order to pursue the kind of professional career he envisions. His parents had paid the school fees of the boarding school for his stay of several years in advance. Vatter, the cocky youngster, arranges a meeting with the director of the school and negotiates with him, that he will get out the school fees already paid by his parents, if he proves that he will be admitted to the Commercial School in Neuchâtel and will be able to take a diploma there. This is the story of Vatter, who even as a young man already has clearly in mind, what he wants. Where his place is. And keeps at it. And achieves what he sets out to do. After his diploma in Neuchâtel, Vatter completes an apprenticeship as a cheesemaker. To prepare carefully his envisioned career as a cheese and milk trader. He succeeds to establish a good reputation in the region in no time at all. At a sufficient distance from his father and his father's business. He leases cheese dairies. Trades in milk and cheese. Takes on offices in the association. As a young man he already made it. One of the dairies he leases, is in Egolzwil in the Canton Lucerne. Egolzwil is a neighbouring village to his native Dagmersellen. Where his father resides. He decides to settle personally in Egolzwil, All inhabitants of Egolzwil are Catholics. Vatter and his family are Protestants. Vatter is openminded and doesn't mind to settle as a Protestant among Catholics. He stirs up a hornet's nest. The Catholic inhabitants of Egolzwil can't and wouldn't understand, that a Protestant, of all people, takes over the local dairy. With his cosmopolitan, jovial manner, Vatter convinces the inhabitants of Egolzwil, that even a Protestant can process their milk and make good cheese. It helps, that the inhabitants of Egolzwil know, that Vatter is the eldest son of the rich and renowned cheese and milk merchant from Dagmersellen. Vatter soon has convinced the inhabitants of Egolzwil of his skills. When Vatter is new, but already accepted in Egolzwil, he sits with his employee on the little bench in front of his dairy on the village's main street after work and smokes a Toscanelli Cigar. A pretty young woman walks by. Vatter looks after her with shining eyes. His employee murmurs, that he must put this woman out of his mind. She is of a better family and has got a taste of the bigger world. She has other ideas, then falling in love with a villager. Besides, she is a Catholic, like all the people in the village. So he, the Protestant has to forget about her. Moreover, there is a rumour that this young woman's father's farm is indebted. Her father, instead of taking care of his wainwright business and his farm, were always hanging around with the factory owner Straehl from the neighbouring town Zofingen at the pile-digger excavations in the Wauwiler Moos, adjacent to his farm. He were a respected person in the community, enjoyed a good reputation, and was an honorary orphan bailiff. But he were a Catholic and probably had a hump full of debts. - Vatter caught fire for the young woman, Nänne. Despite all the obstacles, they married in 1904. Not in Egolzwil and not in Dagmersellen. But in far off Lugano, in the Canton Tessin, where one of Vatter's brothers was currently in position and organizes a dignified wedding on the smallest scale. Far away from the families of Vatter and Nänne. Vatter's family is horrified, that their eldest son is marrying a Catholic, of all people, and above all without a considerable dowry. Nänne's family looks past the stigma of religion, after Vatter takes over his father-in-law's debts. Vatter's trade flourishes. Three daughters are born to the couple, each three years apart.

Vatter, but above all Nänne, is annoyed that the Catholic priest in Egolzwil is constantly imploring her to have her daughters baptized as Catholics, otherwise she and the daughters are threatened with purgatory. Vatter looks around for a new place with less prejudices and more openmindedness to expand his business and to settle. Nänne and Vatter find the perfect estate in Oberrohrdorf in the District Baden in the Canton Aargau. The place consists of an ideal manorial house with grounds, stables, a brush factory, gardens, farmland, woods and vineyards. And Vatter can lease the local dairy. Like in Egolzwil all the inhabitants of the small village Oberrohrdorf are Catholics. But less prejudived then the ones in Egolzwil. No sooner has the young family settled in Oberrohrdorf than local elections are due to be held. Because the newcomer Vatter is a well-to-do and respected man and because there are no other new candidates for the office of municipal councillor, Vatter, although a Protestant and a newcomer in the village, is asked to stand for election. In 1912, Vatter, as the only the Protestant man in the village and as a newcomer, is elected as a municipal councillor. From 1922 to 1941 he is even mayor and a respected personality, who is in demand on municipal, regional, cantonal and national committees. Vatter usually listenes and is known to be a man, who doesn't say more then necessary. But when he opens his mouth, what he says is well-founded. Except when he grumbles. He still grumbles now, as an old man. Lately, for instance, to the new waitress at the Leuen Inn. I am witness, how he tries to explain to her, that the packet of his beloved Toscanelli Cigars, that he orders from her and she brings to him, cost 85 centimes as ever. And not 95 cents as she now suddenly pretends. With a quick glance to the confused waitress, the owner and host of the Leuen Inn gives a sign to her, to come quickly back to the counter to him. He whispers to her, that if the Mayor hadn't realized that the price of his beloved Toscanelli Cigars, which are especially kept at stock for him, had augmented, they didn't argue, just charged the old price. The Mayor were otherwise the most generous man in all matters and gives generous tips. He never hesitates to help out with considerable sums of money, as soon as people were in real need. Nänne shares Vatter's generosity and popularity with the people in the area. Nänne is called 'Nänne' by the people, just as Vatter is called 'Vatter' or 'Mayor'. Nänne is aware of her duties as the wife of a mayor and unobtrusively, as if casually, takes care of people in the community who are in need. Nänne is influenced above all by her cosmopolitan parents' home in Egolzwil. Although she grew up in the countryside without the slightest urban airs and graces, her parents imparted to her the joy and respect for culturally valuable old things, for art, literature and beauty, and also curiosity about everything that crawls and flies. Growing up in a stately farmhouse, she became acquainted with art, valuable antiques, an impressive library and souvenirs from all over the world at the home of her godfather, the manufacturer Gustav Straehl, in his noble villa in Zofingen. Gustav Straehl had been a friend of her father. Gustav Straehl and her father were crazy about the pile dweller excavations in the Wauwiler Moos and spent a lot of time at the excavations and knew every publication about pile dweller excavations in Switzerland. Through her godfather, she gains an insight into upper middle-class lifestyle. So, she is determined to break out of the small world of Egolzwil, not to help in the farmyard, as is customary in peasant families, until a farmer asks her to marry him. She wants to learn a trade and go out into the big wide world. It is important for her to stand on her own two feet and lead a free life. Not to be financially dependent on her parents or a husband. She learned the then respected profession of a ‚Hallentochter' (head waitress) in the noble Spa Hotel Schloss (castle) Brestenberg on the shore of the Lake Hallwyl. With her own money she can indulge her passion for literature and buy a small library. Then she meets and falls in love with Vatter. She marries him against her parents' wishes. Proves her independence. But she doesn't get conceited. After her marriage, she seeks reconciliation with her parents, her parents-in-law and Vatter's siblings. She wins the hearts of all those close to her with charm. Soon she goes on educational trips with Vatter's sisters to Florence, Paris, Heidelberg, visits museums with them, which is rather unusual in their circles. Vatter thinks this fuss about art is women's stuff, but lets his wife have her way. Nänne, smiling mischievously, admonishes Vatter that she is not dependent on his generosity. After all, she earns her own money by raising chickens, keeping bees and selling vegetables and fruit she cultivates in her garden. - I admire this down-to-earthness and this rootedness in and on the countryside with all its openness to the whole world. Perfect material for a novel!"

"Don't you dare drag Nänne and Vatter's life into the public domain in a novel!", Gret acknowledges Hans Günther's narration with a fierce outcry that makes Peter wonder. "We are a decent family!", she adds.

Peter observes how Gret is embarrassed by her violent reaction, barely out. She avoids Hans Günther's gaze, who sits there like a wet blanket because of Gret's reaction, and does not know how he should now react in turn. Silence reigns. Which is icy. But just before the ice melts. What is still missing is a tiny increase in temperature to cause the ice to break.

"Gret, I'm amazed," Peter exclaims, "you love novels and Hans Günther has told us the story of Nänne and Vatter so vividly, as only someone who comes from outside can grasp and reproduce it ..."

"Yes, but ...", Gret blurts out. Hans Günther takes her hand, leads it gently to his lips, presses a kiss on it, then directs his lips to Gret's lips.

The love between Gret and Hans Günther is manifest. Gradually, the difficulties, that are part of a refugee's everyday life, trickle through to Peter, Gret and Gret's family. This in turn brings Peter spontaneous visits from Gret to his office.

"Hans Günther has just received a letter from the Migration Department in Aarau. It's outrageous and absolutely infuriating, a shame, how our country treats valuable foreigners! Hans Günthers residence permit has been extended. But the extension is no longer one year, only five months. Morover the permit now is titeled 'Erstreckung der Frist zur Ausreise aus der Schweiz' (extension of the delay to leave Switzerland). He works here. He holds down the fort in the clinic as a doctor, while the Swiss doctors at the clinic are in the military. And now the open threat that he can be expelled from here any time! Peter, you absolutely have to call Government Councillor S. in Aarau and ask him whether things are being done properly, whether they are still in their right mind at the Migrations Department. He must cancel this ignominious decision at once!"

In Gret's presence, Peter calls Government Councillor S.. S. admits that he is just as outraged by the latest turn of events. The instruction comes from the Federal Migration Departement in Bern and is based on a new law.

He, S., is powerless in this matter, he can't do anything about it. So Gret and Peter have no choice but to make Hans Günther feel, that they stand fully behind him. Pulling their legs out to secure his stay in Switzerland. Nänne and Vatter are in on it, too. Chief K. also declares, that to fight for Hans Günthers stay in Switzerland is a humanitarian cause and in the interest of the Königsfelden Clinic. He does his best and pulls strings, so far without further success. Again, Peter is amazed at how Hans Günther seems to keep his cool in everyday life and doesn't let his colleagues and the clinic staff notice his turbulence.

A Swiss colleague of Peter and Hans Günther in the Königsfelden Clinic expresses behind Hans Günther's back in a circle of colleagues the thought, that B. were an enigma as a person and especially as a German and that the suspicion cannot be dismissed out of hand, that B. could be a young German Nazi ready for action. This loose saying spreads in no time as rumour and fact, that Doctor B. is a deliberate offshoot of the German National Socialists in Switzerland. The rumour also reaches Peter. Peter informs Hans Günther about the rumour. Hans Günther explodes. He tells Peter, in a calmer tone of voice, but still urged on by his inner agitation, that he will confront this colleague and demand from him a correction, an apology and an explanation for his degrading assertion. Peter tries to relax the situation. He casually and grinningly throws as a joke the rhetorically meant question at Hans Günther, "How is it, are you or aren't you actually a young German Nazi ready for action?" Now Hans Günther's collar bursts. In his tension, he doesn't understand Peter's joke. He seems to seriously believe that Peter, whom he considers a friend and confidant, now also distrusts him and implies such an absurd thing. Peter has the greatest difficulty in calming down Hans Günther and convincing him, that his remark was a joke. He apologizes.

"Nevertheless, Hans Günther, I understand your violent reaction. But you must get into the habit of reacting to such and similar questions with cheerful composure. Either in a cynical way, e.g. with a 'but of course, I have never made a secret of my party affiliation and haven't I always worn the party badge openly on the lapel of my jacket?', or in a disarming way with a, 'if that were the case, I would have had to win you over to the Nazis long ago!' The fact that you get so flustered is, well, additionally suspicious to third parties. Think about it."

Peter hopes that the shocked Hans Günther will regain his footing in reality and not hold anything against him for his thoughtlessly uttered remark. As soon as Hans Günther is out of his office, he goes to Gret to tell her about his misstep and to ask her to influence Hans Günther not to hold it against him, Peter.

Peter suspects that something is wrong with Hans Günther. Lately, although he is friendly as shit when they run into each other, he noticeably avoids him, Peter. These actual shadow fights with Hans Günther, whom he regards, according to the circumstances, not only as a good colleague with whom he can maintain friendly relations, but as a brother-in-law-to-be, are a challenge for Peter. A person who is unintentionally far from home and unwelcome by the authorities of the country, where he has ended up, and has to see for himself how to survive, is caught in a dynamic storm of emotions which, in addition to the actual difficulties of worrying about work and everyday life, causes constant unrest, doubts and fears which, due to an exceptional situation, are well-founded. Peter gradually begins to see

Hans Günther's person through different eyes. While Gret, in her grounded, relaxed way, notices the change in Hans Günther, but believes his words and does not question them further, the professional is stirring in Peter. In his ‚déformation professionelle', he immediately thinks of an incipient depression, when Hans Günther develops the habit to withdraw. Gret waves it off. Peter need not worry about Hans Günther. He were simply too busy to have time for social intercourse. She also feels it. She understands his way of functioning. Hans Günthers psychiatric reports for the courts keep him extremely busy, and after all, his reports are so outstandingly good as he shows above-average commitment. That takes time. In addition, as a perfectionist, he also needs an awful lot of time for the periodical of the clinic, Autumn Greetings. And in his spare time - well, one simply has to admire someone who has so much energy - he researches a former refugee from Germany to Switzerland in the first half of the 19th century, August Ludwig Follen, to write an essay for the ‚Medizinische Wochenzeitschrift' (Medical Weekly). So, it is nothing but logical, that she has to take a back seat. She is happy to do so, when she sees how he is truly absorbed in his work and distracted from his real problems as a German refugee in wartime here in Switzerland.

Peter doubts, if, as Gret believes, Hans Günther's condition is truly balanced. He approaches Hans Günther and tells him, that Bertie were meeting up with girlfriends in Zurich. He were, as a father, naturally obliged to be at home and look after little Peider. Would Hans Günther happen to have nothing better to do and be able to keep him company? Hans Günther dodges around for some time, struggles to find excuses, blames work overload and the new issue of the peridocal Autums Greetings, only to resignedly give in to Peter's urging after a while.

Peter has set everything up perfectly. Bertie is up to ask Gret, if she could babysit during her absence. Peter tells Bertie, that he of course will be looking after little Peider. That he will be staying at home because Hans Günther has announced, that he might drop in on an urgent matter. He pretends not to know, what Hans Günther could proably want. Therefore, he does not want to have Gret at home to look after Peider. After all, he as the father can look after his little son as well.

"No, no, don't bother, my dear Bertie. You don't need to prepare anything. Maybe Hans Günther won't pass by. Maybe what he wants to discuss, will be said quickly. And if he should still remain seated, your husband, who is not versed in household matters, will find all the same two glasses, a bottle of wine and even a corkscrew."

As soon as Bertie is out of the house and the maid has put little Peider to bed on the instructions of Peter, Peter tells the maid, she can go home. He will manage on his own. Then he sets out two champagne glasses and salted pretzels on the salon table. Fetches a bottle of Nebiolo Spumante from the cellar, which he knows Hans Günther likes. After all, Hans Günther had once brought this bottle and another bottle of it as guest gifts. He puts the bottle in the ice bucket and waits until the doorbell rings.

Hans Günther seems distracted, apologizes, he just didn't have much time and only could keep Peter company for a short while, as much as he would like to stay with him for the whole evening. „Is Peiderlein already in bed? I have this little gift for him.Will you hand it to him tomorrow?" On entering the parlour, Hans Günther's gaze first falls on the ice bucket and the bottle in it, as Peter notes with satisfaction.

"Peter, how do you know that Nebiolo Spumante is my absolute favourite wine!!!", exclaims Hans Günther, beaming and visibly delighted at the surprise.

Gret, Peter and Bertie can't understand, how a person of good taste can ‚love' such a sweet beverage. The name ‚Nebiolo Spumante' meanwhile became to them a catchword or metaphor for bad taste. They hide this fact from Hans Günther and only use it behind his back. If they drink sparkling wine, then it has to be French Champagne.

Despite his surprise at seeing the Nebiolo Spumante, Hans Günther shows the clear intention to leave quickly. Peter wants to thwart Hans Günther's intention. He points out, that Hans Günther should sit down and at least have one glass of Nebiolo Spumante. He counts on Hans Günther's well-manneredness. Hans Günther refuses to sit down, as he only could stay here for some minutes. But he accepts a glass of Nebiolo Spumante. And a second one. With the third one he even sits down, begins to eat a pretzel, relaxes and gradually – Peter fetches the second bottle of Nebiolo Spumante from the cellar – relaxes. Loses then suddenly his composure.

For the first time, Peter experiences how Hans Günther, who is usually so brisk and always cheerfully upbeat, if he is not, as rarely happens, exploding, shouting and putting on a show of a special kind, collapses inside. He sits there like a heap of misery. Pours glass after glass into himself and starts to grumble, to scold and really get angry.

"I am a failure. A total failure. Here I am getting drunk - and I don't know what to do. Vatel, up there in heaven, can triumph. I fail totally. You should have known Vatel. I can never hold a candle to him! Here I'm treated like dirt and I can't stand up to it. I'm too weak, too cowardly, I don't know... Vatel wasn't like the fathers here. He didn't think much of effeminacy. Vatel had been in the field as a medical officer in a tight-fitting uniform. How I had admired him. At the same time, envied that he had been allowed to go to war, the Great War. My friends and I had maps of Europe, on which we recorded the progress of the German armies and the positions of Germany's enemies. Mottl had been so proud of me, the boy who seemed to be growing into a real and defensible man. When I was asked as a little boy, what profession I would like to take up when grown up, my answer came out like a cannon shot: 'General Field Marshal von Hindenburg!' Anything feminine was frowned upon. Not to mention that Mottl and my friends' mothers would have laughed at us, if we as boys had been interested in chick stuff. My parents, although in the small Silesian town of Jauer, had an urban, middle-class household with a strict regime that seemed natural to me as a child. I grew into this strictness. Intimacies, exchanges of affection with adults, had been frowned upon. Mottl, who came from a family of textile manufacturers that had still been rich in her childhood, knew all about cultivated lifestyles. She even explained to Vatel, whom she adored and to whom she was thoroughly devoted, what was and was not proper in a refined way of life. Vatel had always laughingly emphasized that he came from humble origins, actually were a proletarian man married to an aristocratic woman. Of course, even then I could hear Vatel's mockery, irony and cynicism. Vatel's father,

Grandfather Gustav, had also been a factory owner. With quite successful phases in his business. At that time Vatel had been taught at home by a private tutor, a Fräulein von Stein. Officials approached Grandfather Gustav, the owner of a zinc smelter in the Austro-Hungarian Empire, to offer him a title of nobility in return for an appropriate donation. Grandfather Gustav rejected the request out of hand. Grandfather Gustav, whom Vatel had always experienced as irascible and authoritarian, registered Vatel as an apprentice at a bank without consulting Vatel after his graduation from high school. After all, the eldest son had to take over his father's business in the future. Vatel rebelled. He had other plans. It took him a hard struggle until he was finally able to study at university. Vatel would have preferred to follow his inclinations and study history. As a realist, he knew that with a history degree, only an academic career would have been an option for him. As a professor at a university, his earnings would be too low to be able to support a family appropriately. As a professor, one would have to have a family fortune at one's disposal. Grandfather Gustav's business was not going well at the time. Vatel knew that he could not count on a family fortune, from which he could have drawn. Vatel had to give up his dream of becoming a history professor. He had to see to it, that he could financially stand on his own two feet as quickly as possible. And he had to reckon with the fact that he would probably have to finance the education of his younger brothers as well. Medical school was at that time the shortest course of study and lasted four years. Immediately after graduation, he would be able to open his own doctor's office and earn good money. Nolens volens, Vatel decides to study medicine. Vatel got his way. In 1895, not quite 24 years old, opened his own doctor's office in the small Silesian town of Jauer. His doctor's office runs well from the start. Vatel is able to support his parents and his brothers according to their needs and wishes. He makes it possible for Grandfather Gustav to have the things he considers worthy of his status, but can no longer afford himself. At the turn of the century, for example, Vatel gives Grandfather Gustav the latest model of typewriter, a writing instrument with a rotating ball head, and then a gold pocket watch with the latest marvel. And Mottl's family! Mottl always keeps her composure. Nothing can shake her. Do you think she once complained about the covetousness of her father-in-law, Grandfather Gustav! She always counterbalanced the mockery, the irony, the cynicism of Vatel with calm composure. She never let on, that and how she was suffering. And she must have suffered and is suffering all the more now. Whereas here I lose my composure altogether. Mottl's family on her mother's side had made it to considerable wealth in the grain trade and with oil presses until, after the marriage of her mother, grandmother Rosalie, to a wealthy textile manufacturer, grandfather Jacques, on the occasion of the Vienna stock market crash, her grandfather Jonas loses his entire fortune and dies of a heart attack. Grandfather Jacques, Mottl's father, dies of cancer at the age of 43, when Mottl is 14. The well-run business has to be sold. The children are given a guardian. Mottl knows that as a young woman without a substantial dowry, she has no chance of finding a suitable husband. She will stay with her widowed mother. She is all the more delighted when a young doctor from the small town of Jauer and of good family, Vatel, discovers her sitting in a box at the theatre in Breslau, falls in love with her and asks for her hand in marriage. Vatel earns a handsome living with his practice. He slips into various honorary posts as a doctor and enjoys an excellent reputation as a physician in the region. Vatel and Mottl travel extensively. Vatel is one of the first in the small town to have an automobile, shortly before the Great War. Back then, when buying a car, the buyer got the driving licence for free. So, much to Mottl's dismay, the technophile Vatel gets behind the stearing wheel of his car himself. Vatel's driving skills manoeuvre his car and its contents into a ditch. The passengers survive the overturning of the car. Were only slightly injured. After this car accident the coachman, who is still in the family's service, is converted into a chauffeur. Mottl breathes a sigh of relief. Not much changes for her. For the coachmen, now the chauffeurs, traditionally have a pronounced tendency to the maids in the household. Which clearly goes against Mottl's moral ideas and is to be stopped if possible. A daughter is born to the couple, Ilse. Eight years later they also have a son, I. Now that Grandfather Gustav has been dead for two years, Mottl and Vatel, who were born Jews, feel the need to follow their inclinations and have themselves, their little daughter and me, the newborn, baptized. Also, and not least, to pave the future way into society for me. Anti-semitism has always been there. Brush up your Harry Graf Kessler's Rathenau biography. Then comes the Great War. Mottl and Vatel subscribe their entire fortune in war bonds. Following the call ‚Gold I gave for iron', Mottl, with a heavy heart, donates her valuable family jewellery to finance the war. Then she is plagued by a guilty conscience, because she has kept back her favourite piece of jewellery, a valuable pearl necklace with a magnificent lock. With a heavy heart, she goes to the office to donate this necklace as well. The official's decision is, "Madam, pearls are not gold, cannot be melted down, you can keep your necklace without worry." Around the same time, Vatel reads a notice in the newspaper that the Crown Prince's Palace in Berlin had been burgled and a valuable collection of gold snuff boxes had been stolen. Vatel acknowledged this news with a cynical grin and the saying, 'quod licet Jovi non licet bovi' (what is allowed to Jupiter, is not allowed to ordinary cattle) . Vatel's practice is closed during the Great War. After the war, Mottl and Vatel are left with nothing. They mourn the empire. They cannot come to terms with the new political times. They fear total collapse and Bolshevism. Vatel has barely resumed his practice and is once again prosperous, so that their accustomed lifestyle is not endangered. Ilse and I are amused that Vatel, as a person of respect, has three reserved box seats in the Lutherian Friedenskirche (church) in Jauer, each seat reserved excusively for him with his visiting card for him: as a member of the Officers' Society, as a member of the Medical Society and as a private person. Whenever the practice permits, large trips are made in Europe. On the grounds that Vatel, who is unable to drive, must be able to drive to doctor's appointments and to see patiens at their home in the evening when the chauffeur is not on duty, a special official permission is obtained for me to get my driving licence at the age of 16. Ilse gets her way and doesn't have to sit idle at home until she finds a husband. She is allowed to learn a trade. For Vatel it is clear that the only apprenticeship that can be taken in consideration for his daughter is an apprenticeship as a medical assistant in his own doctor's practice. Ilse rebels. Much to the dismay of Mottl and Vatel. They don't understand their against all need and good sense rebellious daughter any longer. Ilse prevails. As being the first woman to do a banking apprenticeship she receives quite a lot of attention by the local media,. Her banking apprenticeship at the Regional Savings Bank Jauer results in her marrying the bankdirector. Her husband is enthusiastic about technology and drives a sports car, which impresses me in particular. I adopted the political stance of Vatel and also Mottl. I made sure to do everything that promotes my manliness. I do athletics to the point of exhaustion. Besides that, I write poems, often with patriotic content. I am quite successful with my poems. I can recite poems at soirées and publish two volumes of poetry in a Leipzig publishing house. After graduating from high school, I would have preferred to study German and history. Vatel, however, fears that the increasingly strong anti-semitism, now coupled with racial doctrine, could also have detrimental consequences for me, his offspring. He therefore advises me to study medicine out of common sense. Doctors are always and everywhere needed. I let myself be convinced. As a student, I indulged in shooting and horse-riding, much to Vatel's delight, and, following the fashion of young people, joined hiking groups. Influenced by my childhood impressions of the Great War and Vatel in his impressive uniform, I joined the ‚Stahlhelm' (steel helmet), a conservative association of former front-line fighters. In the political wrangling between Bolshevists and National Socialists, the ‚Stahlhelm' clearly leans towards National Socialism, which for me is the lesser evil. Bolshevism, which is highly rampant, especially among intellectuals, must be fought with all means. With the election of Hitler as Reich Chancellor, it very quickly becomes apparent that the Nazis are also targeting Vatel's practice. Vatel has reached a certain age and has his sheep in the dry, so it is not too bad for him to give up his well-run practice, where the health insurance companies no longer reimburse 'Jewish' doctors for patient costs incurred. He and Mottl turn their backs on the small town Jauer, where they go from being respected by everyone to becoming a social hot potato. They move from the small town into hiding as ostracised Germans in the anonymity of the big city Breslau. Where they still could enjoy the extensive cultural offerings enormously.

I remained loyal to the "Stahlhelm" until 1935, when I was expelled as a non-Aryan. Now I am stranded here. Unwanted, hostile. And at home my people go to the dogs, and I'm stuck here, unable to do anything. I have to make sure that I don't drown. But that would be the least evil. What will become of Mottl, of Ilse, of Pimmer, of Trautel at home in Silesia! And here I am, powerless, up to my neck in the floods and can do nothing. Nothing! You understand, with the equipment I brought with me from my beloved Germany, I am not in a position to fight the freedom-loving Confederates, as I am realizing with increasing horror. I have finally lost the strength and motivation to do so," Hans Günther adds dryly.

Then Hans Günthers facial expression changes quickly. He becomes cheerful again. He wants to reach for his glass. But it is empty. Peter hurries to refill it immediately. With a nod, Hans Günther thanks him and empties the glass in one gulp.

"I've made a total fool of myself. Sorry, Peter. Forget what I said. Oh dear, so late already. I apologize for keeping you so long with my bullshit. I hope you don't hold it against me. Man needs hope to keep going. Even if the turns differ fundamentally from his plans and hopes! - And since it seems to be the moment of truth: This Nebiolo Spumante is a horrible swill! The fact that I always pretended to love it so much is pure nostalgia. Vatel had raved about Nebiolo Spumante since his honeymoon in Venice, Italy. He at least pretended, there was nothing better than Nebiolo Spumante. But now, if I remember correctly, at home we always had French champagne or, rarely, German sparkling wine. Vatel probably couldn't or wouldn't buy in Silesia the Nebiolo Spumante, he glorified somehow. His inclination to spakling wines earned Vatel the title of 'Champagne Uncle' among my cousins. Anyway, I thank you. I don't want to strain your hospitality any longer."

Peter keeps his mouth shut. He tells neither Bertie nor Gret about Hans Günther's confession and his brief moral cave-in. Hans Günther also never comes back to what he had confided in Peter. But Peter senses that something has changed for the better in their relationship. And Hans Günther is clearly in a better mood again. And Gret states to Peter after a few days, "Hans Günther is back to his old self. I had always said, that his bad mood was due to the fact, that he is a perfectionist and always wants to tackle too many things at once."

One fine day, Gret surprises Peter with the news, not really surprising but dramatically changing the situation, that enough has transpired. She will marry Hans Günther. On the one hand, Peter admires his sister-in-law for her courage. On the other hand, he is surprised at the wording she has chosen for this announcement. And the combative tone. In the conversation that follows, Peter learns that Gret is totally unhooked by the way Hans Günther has to fight over and over again for his residence, his job. Although they loved each other and wanted to marry, he was so decent and reserved that he didn't want to marry under any circumstances and thus put her in trouble as a Swiss woman marrying a German. Now she had told him in no uncertain terms, that she didn't care about the consequences and that she will marry him. Hans Günther, she confesses, had been quite puzzled by this statement. But he will, she is convinced, accept her decision.

Before Peter talks to Bertie about Gret's announcement and before he addresses Hans Günther about this latest development, he talks to the husband of Annie, the middle daughter of the K. Family, Hans. The latter is a clear-headed man and has family connections with renowned lawyers. Hans expresses reservations about Gret marrying Hans Günther at this time and advises Peter to talk Hans Günther into seeking the help of a lawyer for the formalities. Hans immediately recommends his, Hans', brother-in-law, Attorney U. in Bern. Of course, the costs would not be borne by Hans Günther or Gret. He, Hans, will of course pay for everything.

Attorney U. informs Hans Günther of the devastating legal practice, that links the right of residence of a Swiss woman, married to a foreigner, to the right of residence of her foreign husband. In plain language, this means that a foreigner married to a Swiss woman enjoys no advantages with regard to his residence status. If he is deported, on the other hand, his Swiss wife also loses her right of residence in Switzerland. Under these circumstances, a marriage of Gret and Hans Günther is out of the question, as Gret also realizes. With heavy hearts, they carry on as before. In addition to Chief K. and Peter, the political heavyweight Vatter now vehemently lobby the Migration Departments in Aarau and Bern for Hans Günther to remain in Switzerland.

Mottl in Breslau is not allowed to continue employing her long-time Aryan maid. As a 'Jew', she has to accommodate in her 'Jewish flat' fellow 'Jews' (non-Aryan Christians) who have lost their homes. Then she loses her 'Jewish flat' and has to move in another 'Jewish flat' of friends, cramped together with other 'Jews'. She is finally deported to a collective camp for non-Aryan Christians, where she lives in a small room with other prisoners in the Grüssau Monastery near Landeshut. Hans Günther tries to obtain an entry permit for Mottl to Switzerland. Hans Günther's request is supported by Nänne and Vatter, who agree to take Mottl in at the K. Home in Oberrohrdorf. Against a deposit of 10'000 francs, the entry permit is granted. With an income of 200 francs a month, Hans Günther is unable to pay the deposit from his own funds. Nänne and Vatter step into the breach via Gret and advance the money. Mottl's departure from Germany is delayed for formal reasons set in Germany.

Hans informs Peter that he has heard from Attorney U., his relative, that the legal practice in Switzerland regarding Swiss women married to foreigners has changed. A Swiss wife married to a foreigner now retains her independent residence in Switzerland, even if her husband is deported. This removes for Gret and Hans Günther the obstacles to marriage. In addition, Hans Günther is expatriated from Germany. Is now stateless. Cannot be deported anywhere. Gret and Hans Günther can marry and have a real wedding. Because of the war and because of the worries about Hans Günther's remaining family in Germany, the celbration is kept on a very small scale. At the Registry Office in Windisch with Peter and Edwin F. as witnesses. Then the church ceremony, conducted by Pastor Victor Maag, formerly pastor in Mellingen, a small town neighboring Oberrohrdorf, and now at the Predigerkirche (church) in Zurich, in the Grossmünster Chapel (chapel of the cathedral) in Zurich. Followed by a meal at the Hotel Storchen on the shore of the River Limmat in downtown Zurich, invited by Vatter and Nänne.

FATHER AND SON OVER THE COURSE OF 40 YEARS

4.

Hans Günther is beside himself with joy. On 3 December 1945, Gret, his beloved ‚Scheusälchen' (little monster), his Golden Pheasant, gives him the much longed-for and long-desired offspring and son Rainer. Named after Rainer Maria Rilke, Hans Günther's poet idol. A healthy, strapping boy. Born by chance on the birthday of Hans Günther's beloved Vatel. If Vatel could have lived to see this grandson, Hans Günther spontaneously thinks. The longed-for son means something like a new home and perspective for Hans Günther. Rainer is Swiss by birth, because he cannot get citizenship from his stateless father. He is Hans Günther's future and proof that life goes on, in spite of what had been. Into a wonderful future. The joy in the whole family is enormous. Hans, Gret's brother-in-law and husband of her middle sister Annie, is an obstetrician and takes exemplary care of mother and child in the hospital in Menziken. Hans Günther writes in his diary on 3 December 1945 with a puffed chest and full of pride:

> *So, I have a son! Infinitely happy and grateful. Rainer will be his name. At work, I am not at all concentrated. Dentist. Keller & Hofmann for Rainerlein's birth announcement cards, ready for tomorrow morning. !!!! Happy - happy - happy - happy - happy!!!!*

The next day, Hans Günther jumps on an express train during his lunch break and makes a pilgrimage to Zurich, foregoing lunch with his colleague in the clinic's doctors' dining room. In Zurich, in spite of his not exactly rosy financial situation, he plunges proudly and exuberantly into a noble jewellery shop. Picks out a pretty gold bracelet, which he buys for his ‚Scheusälchen'. Amuses himself by imagining how his colleagues in the clinic, once again, would shake their heads at his extravagances. If they suspected what he has now done. He comes back to work, as if nothing had happened. He is terribly unfocused and full of joy. The question as to why he was absent from lunch is answered with a grin and a muttering of well, well, well ... The colleagues cast conspiratorial glances at each other and one of them says, "The new father, ah! " In the meantime, Hans Günther can't wait until he will travel to Menziken after work to surprise his beloved Gret with the golden bracelet in the hospital and to marvel at Rainer, his offspring and tribe holder.

By chance, while looking through papers, Hans Günther comes across the scanty notes of the beginning of the novel 'Schattenkämpfe' (Shadow Fight(s)), which had been the discharge of a tormented soul six years ago. In it he tries to describe his first steps as a refugee in the foreign country. Hans Günther is so fed up with the old rubbish that he tears up the few handwritten pages and throws them in the wastepaper basket. From now on he absolutely does not want to think about the past. He doesn't care any longer about what had not only been, but had been totally hard to bear. To protect his new family from evil memories and happenings. His transfiguring thoughts about history must be aimed at the time before the lives of Hans Günther and his loved ones had come apart at the seams. He has to make sure that his little prince still gets a glimmer of the ideal world from which his father originated. Hans Günther spontaneously fantasises how later, when he himself has long since been buried and decayed, Rainer, for example, who has long since become an old man, will, from the perspective of a free spirit, use these notes to piece together his, Hans Günther's life, fragmentarily and absolutely inadequately into a satire or a novel, that can hardly capture the full force of what actually had happened. Which Hans Günther now has to suppress in order to survive. This daydream exhilarates Hans Günther immensely and gives him a laughing fit. Let others engage in shadow fight(s). He wants to take care of his little prince in the here and now with the illustrious goal, vivat crescat floreat (he may live, grow, flourish).

Hans Günther has to realize that wanting the best for his offspring and actually managing to give him the best and only the best, so that he may flourish perfectly, are two different pairs of shoes. It is always banal things that get in the way of his happiness, he has almost achieved. There always is something to spoil it. His happiness could be perfect, if there was not, for example, the question of the housing.

Despite an early application, the clinic management couldn't offer him a suitable appartment for a small family with a small child on the clinic grounds. So, Hans Günther is condemned to continue living in his private room between patients wards in the clinic. His room is connected with a second room, that was accorded to Gret and him after the wedding. Gret worked on as a laboratory assistant until the birth of the child. The two rooms had neither a kitchen, nor a private bathroom or toilet. This situation is not at all suitable for a couple with a small child. Peter, who meanwhile has succeeded Chief K. als head doctor of the clinic, tries his best to find a suitable flat or living accommodation for Gret, Hans Günther and the child in one of the many buildings in the Königsfelden park. It turns out to be impossible to find one. So Gret and Rainerlein move in with his parents-in-law, Nänne and Vatter, in Oberrohrdorf until a suitable appartment for the small family is available on the clinic grounds. And Hans Günther is condemned to be weekend father, when he visits his wife and son in Oberohrdorf on free weekends.

Colleague P. had been luckier. With persistent arguments, he had obtained soon after his wedding, by way of exception, permission from the clinic and the Health Department in Aarau to live outside the clinic grounds. He could find and buy a nice and small house in the village of Windisch, in the Wagnerhof Street, close to the clinic, ten minutes by foot. From the beginning his family can live together and enjoy family life.

Hans Günther is annoyed that he had not been more insisting in the housing matter. In retrospect, he is convinced that a solution could have been found, if his demand had been more emphatic. But his good upbringing and his decency forbid him to demand anything vehemently for himself. At the same time he fears to explode, when for him important matters are denied. When he doesn't get, what he absolutely wants, pressure inside him rises and he explodes unvoluntarily, starts to shout in any place, in front of anybody and makes a fool of himself. He feels immensely ashamed afterwards. He must and wants to avoid such explosions at all costs. Couldn't afford and didn't want such an explosion in front of his superiors in the clinic when it came to the housing question. From literature, he is told to

‚Sieh vorwärts, Wener, und nicht hinter dich' (look ahead, Werner, and not behind you). This quotation from Schiller's Wilhelm Tell draws a tail of quotation flashes from Shakespeare behind him. ‚Who is there?', ‚The rest is silence' and so on, until inner peace is back after ‚What are you grinning at me hollow skull'. The turmoil in Hans Günther's head sometimes takes on crazy proportions. Intuitively, however, sitting at his desk, he reaches for the medical files again, in the study of which he had been engrossed, until the mental chatter caused him to digress. Now he wants to read on. Careful, he says to himself, otherwise I'll end up myself in the loony bin with all these crazy thoughts. At the idea of landing himself in a psychiatric clinic, Hans Günther spontaneously bursts out laughing. Which embarrasses him. He immediately looks around fearfully to see if his office colleague P. has noticed his sudden laughter.

The brief glance in P.'s direction makes Hans Günther catch his breath. P. seems so engrossed in his work that he seems not to have paid attention to Hans Günther's laughing fit. P. is floating, Hans Günther shoots through his head, on a pink cloud. Which Hans Günther can certainly relate to. P. and Hans Günther, and also Gret and P.'s wife, had a good laugh when they discovered at the same time in spring, that both, P.'s wife and Gret, P.'s wife for the second time, Gret for the first time, were pregnant. Simultaneously, both children have hatched. Both are sons. P.'s Andreas is born one day after Hans Günther's Rainer.

The idea that Hans Günther had spontaneously associated the pithy P. with a pink cloud amuses Hans Günther. He marvels at how coincidentally the most opposing things, people and circumstances often come together in his mind. He has to memorise this thought with P. and the pink cloud. The thought is too cute. The thought must not plop into the black hole of memory and remain gone forever and ever.

Hans Günther teases P. with the remark, "So, how does it feel to be a newly minted father of a son?". P. looks up from his work. Grins at Hans Günther and shakes his head.

The exuberant joy of the new father Hans Günther gets a damper each time when the little one cries and cannot be calmed. When he, Hans Günther, holds the infant, who shits in his nappies, in his arms in Oberohrdorf. The cleaning of the infant definitely is womens business. Gret rushes over. Hans Günther's vision that his son would catapult him into a perpetual state of happiness turns out to be wrong. The arrival of his son doesn't shrink everything else of the nerve-racking daily routine to negligible tininess, so that it would seem to have disappeared. Hans Günther has to admit, to have had wrong ideas. The illusion of a fatherhood, that gives perpetual happiness, bursts like a balloon. Unvoluntarily   disillusionment   sets   in.   A disillusionment that the newly minted father must not show in the flood of congratulations that suddenly befuddles him. He absolutely does not want to disappoint anyone. Putting a good face on a game that is by no means evil, but nevertheless characterised by sluggish mundanity. Hans Günther fears that the dear people in his immediate environment, who are well-disposed towards him and always support him, will not understand him now that his most ardent wish has come true, if, despite his great happiness, he shows this face, of which three people important to him recently threw at him, independently of each other, "it's always obvious from your expression on your face, when something doesn't suit you." This face, which he shows to others without knowing it and which he does not see himself, betrays him. Obviously, he has trouble applying automatically his motto, always smile, to his actual facial expression.

These people, who do not have to struggle with his difficulties, live an orderly everyday life and do not know, what it is like, when everything goes haywire in the wider environment, which is not perceived by everyone, and the most terrible dramas take place. Hans Günther curses his innate spontaneous inclination to tormenting questioning. He imagines how a simple mind can simply rejoice. Not letting anyone or anything spoil his joy. The thought that he, as a not entirely unsophisticated being, at times twirls himself up in completely twisted ideas, produces an amused grin on his face. Exactly at the moment when his beloved Scheusälchen, his Golden Pheasant, his Gret puts the freshly swaddled, no longer smelly, but pleasantly scented little Rainer back into his arms. At the same time, with a mischievous smile, which Hans Günther gratefully notices, she lets fall, "your blissful smile about your Rainer, which has driven away your often all too serious face expression since he arrived, is my greatest joy, dearest Hansel, and gives me the courage to find my way over all difficulties." Hans Günther knows that he has to show a happy face to his beloved, but after having given birth somewhat fragile Gret. He's happy with the coincidence that he really is smiling at this moment.

As a doctor who, out of inclination, would have preferred to work in the field of gynaecology, but now, following the plight of the refugee from Germany in Switzerland, has ended up in psychiatry, which he initially detested, he diagnosed soon after Rainer was born, with implanted professionalism, a touch of postnatal depression in his wife, who is often in a subdued mood. Has problems breastfeeding. Because of inflamed nipples and has to give up breastfeeding. She is terrified by this. He can't get the accidental discovery out of his head. He keeps the 'diagnosis' to himself, however, and from then on, has to experience how this 'diagnosis' always itches in his memory at every suitable and unsuitable opportunity. He secretly worries about the well-being of his beloved wife. Our happiness, he tells himself steadfastly, is now perfect. Hans Günther makes an effort to beam at his mildly smiling Gret and to feel Rainer's closeness in his arms. To enjoy the moment. Because soon the weekend is over, and he has to make the pilgrimage alone from Oberrohrdorf back to the clinic, where he spends the working week alone in his private room, in his office and on the patient wards.

No reason to mope. Better times will come soon. Soon! After all, he had been lucky all things considered and, as Mottl had written to him several times in her letters, he is a Sunday's child. Hans Günther can be happy as a lark and his beloved Gret thinks practically and, in her undercooled way, is always controlled. Little son Rainer makes a pleasurable gurgling sounds. Hans Günther smiles to him.

Hans Günther bears with composure how his Rainer experiences his first time far away from him. He cannot look at him, how he looks every day and how he changes very, very little, but still constantly. He can only participate in his little son's everyday life when he visits him at weekends or on days when he is off-duty. But then the little family is in the open house of his parents-in-law, Nänne and Vatter, always surrounded by countless people. Hans Günther forbids himself from naggingly questioning the situation, which in itself is ideal under the given circumstances.

Hans Günther's happiness is perfect. He can send to all his friends, relatives and acquaintances, scattered all over the world, the first photo of father and son, saying that now his happiness is perfect. In fact, Hans Günther's happiness is almost perfect. When, on seeing Gret in Oberohrdorf, his secret diagnosis of postnatal depression once again leaps into his memory, he cannot help but share his concern for his beloved Gret with Nänne. The kind, wise, educated, clever Nänne reassures Hans Günther. Greti must first get used to the new situation. It will work itself out. He, Hans Günther, should go to the Leuen Inn with Vatter to take part in his Jass round. Hans Günther is relieved. So grateful that he has been welcomed into this Swiss family with such open arms. In the Leuen Inn, where Vatter insists that he, Hans Günther, not just watch but join in the game of Jass, Hans Günther has to be careful not to accidentally play the wrong cards, lest he be reprimanded by Vatter.

5.

As the eldest of three sisters, Bertie had always felt responsible for her younger sisters. Especially for the youngest, Gret, who is six years younger than her. Vatter, who is constantly busy with his business and with politics in the village, in the region, throughout the country and abroad, and who is also committed to the Free Democrats and to the shooting club and other associations, is not present enough to perceive the true situation. The kind-hearted Nänne thinks her daughters are so special and so successful that she would never dream of telling her youngest to be more diligent and to learn something. This constant worry about the somewhat easy-going Gret, who seems to take nothing in life seriously, has remained with Bertie, even though Gret is now a married woman and mother of a small son. Family is and remains family. Fortunately, Gret now has her Hans Günther, who is a real enrichment to the family.

Peider, Bertie's son, now seven years old, is thrilled that his godmother Gret has a little boy. Considers godmother Gret's Little One, Rainerlein, to be his brother and doesn't let anyone talk him out of this belief. At school, in the first grade, he proudly reports that he has got a little brother. When a pupil in this first grade has a new baby brother or sister, all the pupils in the grade, under the direction of the teacher, sing a beautiful little song in honour of the new arrival. The teacher can't believe that Peider has got a baby brother.

"I met your mother in the village just a week ago. She didn't tell me anything about getting a baby."

"And when I say I have a baby brother. His name is Rainer, and he's very, very small. The Little One."

In order not to disappoint Peider, the teacher makes all the pupils get up and sing the song 'Im Aargäu sind zwöi Lièbi' (In Aargau are two sweethearts) and Peider stands there with a swollen chest and is very happy. The next day, he has to admit to the teacher that his mother had said that the Little One belonged to Godmother Gret and Uncle Hans Günther and was not really his brother. But to him, the Little One is his brother.

Bertie finds the misery of not being able to find a nice flat for the young family on the whole clinic grounds gruesome, and talks to Peter.

"Don't forget, it's your sister-in-law you care so much about, her husband and her little child! It's awful that they must be separated."

"It is precisely because she is my sister-in-law that I, as the head doctor of the clinic, must not turn the world upside down. The interiors of these many newer, old and ancient buildings in Königsfelden are not, after all, designed as family dwellings. Or do you expect me to have a nice little flat made up for them in the crypt of the monastery church!"

"Daddy, I can't argue with you."

"Mommy, you should have noticed this some time ago."

Basically, Bertie is relieved that Gret and the Little One are staying with Nänne and Vatter in Oberrohrdorf for the time being. There Gret, who could quickly become overwhelmed with the Little One, has the necessary help in caring for the infant from Nänne and all the helpful spirits who are always buzzing around the K. Home. With his professional commitments, Hans Günther would have neither enough time nor energy to look after Gret and the Little One. Not to mention that caring for babies is a woman's job. Gret would mostly be alone with the small child during the day, especially in a flat on the clinic grounds. So, from Bertie's point of view, the temporary solution is not necessarily bad.

So that Hans Günther, as a straw widower, doesn't have to mope around too much during the week, she and Peter often ask him to have a glass of wine after dinner, which Peider is delighted about. When Uncle Hans Günther comes, the boy is beside himself. Then Peter and Hans Günther either play chess or Hans Günther and Bertie read the Odyssey together in Greek.

On these occasions, Hans Günther never tires of expressing his amazement at how Nänne and Vatter, despite their rural surroundings in this small village of Oberrohrdorf with pure country life, stand for a cosmopolitanism that seems, in these surroundings a real surprise. How grateful he is, that fate has taken him with his class-conscious, Prussian background to such a wondrous, exotic and emotionally close world for him. Bertie is proud of her origins. She is pleased that Hans Günther correctly assesses her origin.

Then again, he raves about how he can have a wonderful exchange about literature with Nänne. He would have least expected to find a woman here in Switzerland and in the countryside who admires Heinrich Heine, but also knows Börne, Herwegh, Freiligrath and Zschokke. Moreover, she shared his admiration for the German painter Caspar David Friedrich, but could not resist introducing him to the work of the Swiss painter Ferdinand Hodler. She also drew his attention to the artists Cuno Amiet, Helmut Hubacher and Hans Trudel. These artists she knew personally and who, as renowned artists, were in contact with her, the ‚simple woman from the country', as she pleases to call herself. He was completely taken in by this subtle mother-in-law, who knew how to tell pretty stories about everything and everyone. They make the connection to their rural everyday life vivid. The sober Bertie is strangely touched by Hans Günther's exuberance, which borders alarmingly on braggadocio, but at the same time she feels flattered because she thinks he is right to praise her parental home so highly.

Bertie and Peter too are happy that their brother-in-law is so culturally aware. Bertie is also curious about the stories that Nänne has entrusted to Hans Günther. After all, many of these stories were simply lost in ordinary everyday life.

Hans Günther is a gifted storyteller and needs only one cue to get started. When the sculptor Hermann Hubacher wanted to give Nänne a small bronze sculpture, she rejected the beautiful sculpture as a gift and insisted on paying at least the costs of the casting. The casting had cost 6,000 francs. Which she had paid out of her own money. Shaking his head, Vatter then asked what she had paid for the poppet, by which he meant the 'Hubacherin', the bronze sculpture of a standing woman in a Greek-looking floor-length robe. "Well, something like 600 francs," Nänne murmurs. Vatter had been horrified. It was a disgrace that 600 francs were paid for such a poppet, when a farmer's family could buy a calf with that money. Of course, Vatter saw through Nänne's swindle and hummed his horror with a wink and a grin. Nänne loved Vatter for the way he remained grounded in reality, yet respected her actions and let her have her way. Vatter likes to play the grumpy grumbler and tries to cover up his success as a well-connected businessman and doer. His interest in the big, wide world is no coincidence. He learned French as a small child and has always maintained his love for France. After 1871, soldiers from the Burbaki army interned in Switzerland were placed on his parents' farm. The French-speaking soldiers would have had fun with this toddler, Vatter. They tried to teach him some French. The first word Vatter spoke as a toddler was 'pomme' (apple). And the child also struggled with the incomprehensible term 'Pfyffe-Lampe'n Öl' (the nonsensical word 'pipe-lamp-oil' as a Swiss Germanisation of the French 'vive l'empereur', long live the emperor).

Bertie thinks it is essential to write down and record these stories so that they are not lost for the next generation.

"You are now the father of a son, Hans Günther. That's an obligation! And you can write so well. Not only for your little Rainer. Our little Peider and all of us could benefit from it too."

Bertie realizes that Hans Günther had waylaid a good opportunity to have a confidential conversation with her. She is flattered and very curious about what he will confide in her. He fears, he begins to speak hesitantly, that the little son is being pampered in Oberrohrdorf. This is not a criticism of Nänne and Vatter, but he wants his son not to be spoiled too much. Bertie laughs at Hans Günther. Nänne and Vatter are not in the least bit emotional and pampering. She herself is the best example of how soberly and coolly Nänne and Vatter deal with children. When she turned twelve and the question arose where she should attend the district school, which never existed in the small village of Oberrohrdorf, in neighbouring Mellingen or Baden, a district school had just been built and opened in Rothrist, far away from Oberrohrdorf in another part of Aargau. Vatter's very old Godmother had lived in Rothrist at the time. As a single woman and milliner, she had achieved considerable prosperity. Due to the straw hat industry in Wohlen and the surrounding area, hats from the Aargau were in great demand throughout the known and accessible world at that time. As a milliner, Godmother had served customers for hats all over Europe, had travelled after her customers through half of Europe, as it were as an interfering milliner, and had earned a lot of money with it. Godmother then realised that she, as the best taxpayer in Rothrist, was financing the new district school for the most part herself and yet, as an old maid and spinster, had no child who was now attending the school. Her nephew, Vatter, should definitely give one of his daughters to her for care. So that at least one member of the family could enjoy the new district school. So she, Bertie, was separated from her family and placed with the very, very old Godmother and her equally very, very old maid in the stately house on the main street in Rothrist. Bertie suffered terribly from homesickness. At school, she felt morally obliged because the godmother had with her taxes paid for the construction of the school, to take all the free subjects offered, or at least as many of them as possible, in order to profit as much as possible from what the school had to offer, to the satisfaction of Godmother. When it came to the question of who from the her grade wanted to take courses in Latin, later on also in Greek, she felt obliged to come forward. She had not been able to discuss these things with the Godmother or the maid. So, she was the only one in her year who learned Latin and Greek and then graduated from high school. Nänne and Vatter did not understand at all why she was so unhappy in Rothrist. Godmother was very special. Bertie had once seen her reading the newspaper on the small bench in front of the house in the last evening sun. But Godmother was holding the newspaper upside down in her hands. Bertie asked her about it. ‚Godmother, you are holding the newspaper upside down.' Godmother replied gruffly, that it didn't matter. She couldn't see anything anyway with those stupid glasses. And couldn't possibly read the newspaper. ‚Godmother, then we have to go to the optician in town and get you new and better glasses.' Nonsense, replied Godmother. Without glasses, she would be able to read the newspaper just fine. ‚But what do the people in the village gossip about when they see the old hag still reading the newspaper without her glasses!'

Hans Günther is amused by these stories and tales from the family's store of legends. And Bertie adds that he need not worry in the least about little Rainer being pampered by Nänne and Vatter in Oberrohrdorf. They are nice and good people, but you can't accuse them of being sentimental. Bertie's respect for Hans Günther in his role as father increases. He cares about what is to become of his little son. She suspects that he will be present in his upbringing and that he will provide Gret with the necessary support she needs to function well as a mother and to approach her motherhood with the necessary seriousness.

Bertie overhears that Hans Günther has a new worry that distracts him from his concern for his little family. Hans Günther receives the outrageous notification from his bank in Brugg that his money in his Swiss bank account is blocked as 'German property' based on a newly enacted law and that he can no longer dispose of it. Bertie can hardly believe that a now stateless person, formerly German, who had been persecuted in Nazi Germany on racial grounds, is now suddenly treated as a normal German again and as such, after the war has finally ended, is treated as an enemy in neutral Switzerland, as are his assets in Switzerland. Bertie urges Peter and Vatter to stand up for Hans Günther and his money, for God's sake. Both stick up their guns. As tragic and hard to bear as it is, this is the irony of fate, as politics sometimes writes it, and against which the individual citizen is powerless.

One fine day, Hans Günther comes to Bertie with the news that his colleague P. has informed him that a nice three-room flat with an additional attic has become available in a two-family house owned by Master Builder R. in a neighbouring house at Wagnerhof. To Bertie's great astonishment, Peter immediately declared that he would support Hans Günther's application for exception permission to live outside the clinic grounds in Windisch without further ado and that he would lobby the Health Department in Aarau to have it approved. Bertie knows Mrs Master Builder R. and promises that the next time Gret visits Königsfelden, they will visit her together, to have tea with her. That way, the flat is safe for them. Hans Günther can rent the flat for his small family for spring 1947. Bertie and Peter see that Gret and Hans Günther's happiness is now perfect. At last the little family is united. They can lead a normal family life. Peider is beside himself with joy that his brother - he can't be talked out of the fact that godmother Gret's little boy is not his brother - now lives nearby, and he can play with him whenever he wants. Gret also seems to be very excited about the new flat. She proves to be an ingenious interior designer, and soon the flat is homely furnished. Hans Günther has his own kingdom in the attic room. For future visits by relatives from Germany, which will soon be possible again as the borders have just been reopened, the attic room can be used as a guest room.

To welcome his son in the new family flat, Hans Günther, as he tells Bertie, wants to get a cuddly toy for Rainerlein in the toy shop in Brugg. Bertie accompanies him to the toy shop. It has to be something special for his offspring. Not one of those ordinary teddy bears. Hans Günther's gaze wanders over the racks full of soft toys. His gaze involuntarily lingers on a white greyhound. A hard stuffed, slender body made of linen with textile, sparse fur. Bushy, long tail. A hard head elongated into the tip of the nose. Four hard, thin stick legs. Two lumpy floppy ears. Glassy, brown beady eyes. The sight of this stuffed animal awakens old memories in Hans Günther, as he confesses to Bertie, which bring tears to his eyes. Mottl and Vatel had always loved to meet the Liegnitz doctor Paul G. and his wife Erna on the free doctors' afternoon in Liegnitz. Hans Günther had become friends with their son Heino, who was the same age. He often accompanied his parents to these meetings and the joint excursions. Erna G., a very chic and attractive appearance, causes a sensation wherever she appears, also with her magnificent Borzoi, her greyhound. He has to buy this plush greyhound, which reminds him nostalgically of

Erna G.'s Borzoi, for his son. Bertie is somehow proud of her brother-in-law's exclusive taste. She laughs happily.

"This stiff stuffed animal is supposed to be for cuddling! Hans Günther, Hans Günther!"

The Little One twists and turns the stuffed greyhound until he comes across the bushy, cuddly tail. He presses it against him. Holding his stuffed animal by its tail, he drags it around with him, as soon as he can walk on wobbly legs for the time being, in the new flat. In the Wagnerhof. In Windisch.

6.

Gret is blossoming. Finally her own flat. Four walls of her own that she and her small family can live in. She is glad to have escaped from the protection of her parental home, which had been comfortable and had relieved her. Now she can finally organize her everyday life to her own liking. Above all, she can act as a hostess in her own home. She loves company that she can choose and enjoy herself.

Soon she realizes, life is really difficult. She has too many things in mind, she would like to do. There is the Little One for whom she has to be there around the clock. He is cute, thrives splendidly and gives her a lot of joy. At the same time, however, he limits her possibilities to organize her everyday life as she pleases. The proximity to her eldest sister Bertie suits her well. She can leave the Little One with her when she wants to meet friends and acquaintances in Baden or Zurich. At the same time, however, Bertie's Peider is already at school and she cannot always expect her to look after her toddler. Hans Günther, on the other hand, is too busy to find time to take care of the Little One occasionally. Not to mention that Gret soon realizes how little the very enthusiastic and proud father can do with a toddler. Rather, he dreams of all the things he will be able to do with his son as soon as he is bigger and more reasonable.

Gret knows that Prussianism clings to her Hans Günther, the now stateless man, even though Germany has at least been lost to him externally. He does not give up his belief in Germany and the good Germans. She admires that about him. She also encourages him now, after the war, to put aside his almost pathological caution of political involvement in the country, where he still is considered as a refugee, and to join the Neues Deutschland association, which was founded by the refugee Wolfgang Langhoff and is now legal. Admiration for her Hans Günther nevertheless drives Gret into a conflict when she observes how Hans Günther jokingly, but full of irony, talks down to his little son in a Prussian way, with tomboyish severity. But the little boy does not seem to be impressed by Hans Günther's tone. Gret spontaneously thinks it would be nice if the little son developed the gentle manner of Nänne and not the brisk Prussian manner of Hans Günther. This thought irritates Gret. It makes her ponder.

In general, not everything is quite as rosy as Gret had dreamed. The pretty Sunday walks with her husband and pram. The few moments when the three of them are in the living room and Hans Günther and she enjoy the sounds and words or sentence fragments that the Little One utters. When they are visited by friends, relatives and acquaintances. Or when they visit them and proudly show their Little One, who evokes calls of delight. All this does not hide the everyday moments when Gret reaches her limits. When the Little One hardly leaves her alone. When she suspects that Hans Günther is playing over what is bothering him with ironic jokes and cannot or will not tell her what is weighing him down. When Hans Günther is exposed to hostility against Germans, although he hasn't been a German for years. This rarely happens because he is now quite well known and respected as a doctor. But when he is shunned or treated condescendingly because of his origins, Gret suffers with him. When official papers flutter into the house again and Hans Günther is completely flummoxed by the impositions. The many letters Hans Günther receives from friends and relatives scattered all over the world are refreshing. Then he so gladly and masterfully tells how his life used to have been with all the relatives and friends in good old, but now lost to Poland Silesia. This joy in telling and remembering is not even spoiled by the terrible news contained in most of the letters about relatives and friends, who did not survive the persecution, who were murdered in concentration camps. Gret is also powerless in the face of Hans Günther's concern for his sister Ilse and her family, who experienced the end of the war in Silesia, seem to have been driven out of Silesia in 1946, like all Germans, but from whom he has had no news for years because postal traffic with Germany has ceased.

Gret, who is by nature a cheerful and open person, often has to try very hard not to let her head hang down in the face of all the everyday worries. She knows that she has to be a support for Hans Günther during this difficult time for him. She must not show any weakness. Otherwise, he would also let himself go. For her, everyday life often means pressure from too many sides. But basically, she is happy to have her own flat and her small family, which is able to shine even in hard times. She doesn't want to burden anyone around her with her worries and needs. She only dares from time to time to open up to Peter, her brother-in-law. Especially when he won't let up and wants to know how she is doing, not officially, but in reality. This feels good to her and gives her strength. Peter shoos away her worry that she is neglecting the Little One because of all these everyday things by saying that the Little One is growing up to be a lively and quite independent little fellow. That would not be the case if he were neglected.

"Hans Günther can't do too much with toddlers and I, I simply don't have the strength anymore, sometimes ...", it bursts out of Gret.

"No parents are perfect?! Look at the Little One and be happy how he's thriving. Don't rack your brain," Peter encourages her with a smile.

In moments of mental exhaustion, Gret is in a mood where nothing matters any more, where she doesn't care about anything and only wants to find her own balance again. In such moments, she would like to throw in the towel. Give the Little One to Bertie, who makes such a fuss over him. And leave Hans Günther to himself. She would take up her work as a laboratory assistant again, which had fulfilled her so much. Just admitting such thoughts stirs up a guilty conscience in Gret and the feeling of being ungrateful.

Some of Hans Günther's tension eases when mail arrives from Germany from his sister Ilse. The whole family has luckily survived well the expulsion from their home in Silesia, which had been taken by Russians and Poles, and the flight to West Germany. Although the family is separated. The children are housed in school camps in West Germany, and Ilse is separated from her husband. Gret suggests to Hans Günther that he should at least invite the children to Switzerland for a vacation.

"Can we afford it? They have lost everything. We have to feed them up. And rig them up. It will cost."

Gret shakes her head with a smile. She doesn't even need to mention that Vatter and Nänne can always be relied on in financial straits. So in the summer of 1947, Hans Günther's fifteen-year-old nephew, Karl-Heinz, formerly known as Pimmer, whom Hans Günther had not seen for ten years, now a lanky, tall and starved young man, who is getting his first real meal here in Switzerland after the war. Karl-Heinz gets everything he needs and is staying in Windisch and Oberrohrdorf. Much to the delight of little Rainer, who is amazed at the big uncle who suddenly appears, but is supposed to be a cousin, just like Peider. As soon as other people are around - and that is often the case - Gret and Hans Günther no longer count for anything in little Rainer's eyes. Gret is amazed at how fearlessly the little boy approaches strangers with a broad grin on his little face and seems to know no shyness. Hans Günther is visibly happy that he hardly needs to crawl around on the floor with his still incomprehensible, often defiant little offspring and does not have to constantly fend off a little spider monkey that crawls around him at the most impossible times and demands his attention. Hans Günther also mentions to Gret how much satisfaction it gives him that Rainerlein, as a curious little boy exploring the world, is not constantly hanging on to the coat-tails of women who, because he is so cute, merely coddle him.

Gret is alarmed when Hans Günther sits there totally crestfallen after opening his mail, suppresses tears and throws two letters at Gret.

"Read this!", he chokes out in an imperious tone.

One letter, as Gret knows, is from Hans Günther's former primary school teacher in Heidelberg, during the last year of the First World War, when he had started school there. Much to the dismay of Mottl, who finds it hard to accept that her little son has to attend an ordinary public school with boys from all social backgrounds. Hans Günther as a little boy falls somehow in love with his first school teacher and writes letters to her, after the family had left Heidelberg after the war to return to Jauer in Silesia. As a young man Hans Günther studied for one or two semesters in Heidelberg. He keeps in touch with his first school teacher, Miss Maria S. up to now. In he letter now Miss S. strongly advises Hans Günther to forget about returning to Germany. In the present chaotic conditions it were almost impossible to build up an existence as a doctor. The prospects were very poor. It could be a long time before Germany recovered. She bases her advice on countless conversations with doctors in Heidelberg. The second letter is obviously from a professor of medicine, whom Hans Günther had got to know during his semester in Heidelberg. Like Miss S., he also strongly advises against resettling in Germany at this time.

Gret thinks she is dreaming. Hans Günther had never said a word to her about his plans to return to Germany. She is totally shocked that he lets third parties in on his plans before discussing them with her.

"Sorry, Hans Günther, but it simply doesn't work like that. We are a family. You can't just decide for me without asking me what I ..."

"My Golden Pheasant, I didn't want to worry you before I had made sure whether a return to Germany was actually advisable and sensible," Hans Günther presses out with tears in his eyes. "We would have decided together. If you hadn't wanted to, we would have stayed here anyway. As we are staying now. But you have to understand me, with all the commotion always about my residence and work permit here ..."

"Now you can apply for citizenship after all, then everything will be much easier ..."

One day Gret watches in consternation and irritation as Klein-Rainerlein stands on the balcony of the flat for the longest time in the afternoon, his cheeks nestled against the railing, his gaze fixed on what is happening on the Wagnerhof Street in front of the house. She is embarrassed by the way the boy follows the events on the small Wagnerhof Street down there for the longest time. On the street the funeral procession of old Mr. St., called by everybody Father St., who has died in the neighbouring house, is gathering. First the hearse, pulled by two horses, enters the cul-de-sac. It is turned around. Waits. The horses paw restlessly on the gravel of the Wagnerhof Street. Rainerlein stares, watches fascinated. After a while, from the entrance of the neighbouring house at the end of the cul-de-sac, first an incense burner-wielding altar boy in a black cassock with white lace beaf comes up the stairs from the front door of the house up to the garden gate and then to street level, where the hearse waiting. The first altar boy is followed by another altar boy, carrying a wooden cross. Klein

Rainerlein can no longer be removed from his perch by any force. Gret tries several times to lure him back into the flat, with demands, with promises of sweets if he comes in. She threatens, not to love him any more, if he does not finally obey and come into the flat. Her efforts are useless. In the meantime, the priest in his flowing robes comes out of the mourning house and walks up to the hearse. Right behind him, six men in black suits carry the coffin. Behind them follows the mourning family dressed in black. When the funeral procession is composed, it sets off at a deliberate pace to turn from the end of short Wagnerhof Street into Lindenhof Street. The procession is led by the impressive Police Constable R. with his wild moustache and in his impressive uniform and the gleaming helmet, followed by the hearse, pulled by the horses. Behind them the altar boys, the priest and the mourning family. The spectacle the Little One is watching, lasts over an hour. He remains quiet as a mouse the whole time. Gret worries that he sees things he is too small to understand and digest. When in the evening Gret tells Hans Günther of her concern, he says casually in an ironic tone, that anyone with eyes wants to see something. Hans Günther, the specialist in matters of the psyche, can't be persuaded to explain to his little son in an appropriate way, what he has watched the whole afternoon.

Gret is pregnant again. Hans Günther is proud that Rainerlein is getting a sibling.

Hans Günther tells Gret, when he comes home from work one late afternoon, how he has observed his offspring playing in the sandbox in front of the T.'s neighbour's house in T.'s garden with their daughter Hildegard. The moment he noticed the two of them, without them seeing him approach, the two of them crouched in the sandbox as if frozen. Rainerlein stares at Hildegard in horror and disgust. Rivulets of snot run out of Hildegard's nose. Hildegard gleefully catches these streams of snot with her tongue and transports them into her mouth. Hans Günther, who, as he confesses to Gret, is disgusted by this sight, seriously wonders whether this Hildegard is the right company for his offspring. Whether he is not learning things from her that are disgusting. Gret shakes her head at the unworldliness of her Hans Günther.

Gret is pleased that Hans Günther writes a little poem for Bettina's birth announcement: ‚Rainerlein, zwei Jahr allein, hat seit heut ein Schwesterlein' (Rainerlein, two years only child, has got a little sister today). Shortly after Bettina's birth, Hans Günther writes in his diary, which Gret accidentally finds lying open, 'Rainer has been a bit too rambunctious lately. So, I read him Struwwelpeter,   after supper' (Struwwelpeter is the traditional and famous childrens book, written by the doctor and psychiatrist Heinrich Hoffmann in 1844 in Frankfurt). It seems to Gret, that her Hans Günther is overjoyed to have finally a cuddly little girl, which he can spoil. It is not to be trimmed to a masculine ideal like the boy. Hans Günther is be infatuated with the chubby and so sweet little girl, who can be spoilt without harm. To little Rainerlein, who is often defiant and definitely not so nice like his little sister, it is soon clear, that his little sister ist his fathers darling and favourite. Gret is surprised at how little the father's reaction seems to affect the Little One. She worries that little Rainer often torments his little sister. When she starts to cry, he pretends with wide open eyes, that he hasn't touched her. To third parties he openly declares, that his parents should take the crying little thing back to where they got it. He does not need it at all.

The clinic can finally offer the young family a flat on the clinic grounds. In the middle wing of the main building, on the top floor, the third floor. Three huge rooms with a bathroom, private toilets, kitchen and two huge corridors of their own. These rooms, which have been declared private flats, are not contiguous. They consist of two blocks, between which there are publicly accessible rooms. From the first floor a huge stone staircase with about 180 steps first leads to the second floor, where the head doctors very large and pompous private appartment with rich decorated representation rooms and endless corridors is, and then to the thirdfloor. Adjoining and open to the staircase is first on the second floor a huge entrance hall, four meters high, with four huge columns and with a partly glass ceiling, that lets – through the the very large screed above – dim daylight in, as from the staircase as well, as the hall has no windows to the outside, only doors to other rooms. A big door with double wings in the center of one side of the hall gives to the clinic's own huge ballroom with a theatre stage and adjoining functional rooms. On the same side as the big door with double wings, on the two edges to the right and to the left are the two entrance doors to the two blocks of the private flat of Gret and Hans Günther. They are not bothered by the fact, that between the rooms of their private flat is the public accessible big ballroom of the clinic. And the public accessible huge entrance hall. On the contrary, Gret enjoys being part of the pulse of the clinic again. Since Peter, Gret's brother-in-law has been appointed head doctor of the clinic, Bertie, Peter and Peider occupy together with two maids the head doctors appartment on the second floor, one floor below

Gert's and Hans Günther's flat. Gret is sure that the move from the modest three-room flat in the village of Windisch with its attic room to the palatial flat in the middle wing of the main building of Königsfelden will bring significant changes and new perspectives, relationships and connections. The closeness to Bertie and her family is pleasant for Gret on the one hand, but on the other hand, she knows that Hans Günther does not want to be socially absorbed by them and wants to cultivate his own relationships.

7.

Once again, Gloria is almost bursting at the seams with mockery of the oh-so-smart gentlemen of creation when it comes to practical matters. The oh-so-smart gentlemen of creation seem to be so clever that they have a board in front of their heads and don't want to see the simplest solution to a problem. So she, Gloria, the little and inconspicuous secretary of the Königsfelden Clinic, whom nobody really takes seriously, has to make an appearance. Everyone is amazed that she, of all people, comes up with something so clever. And at the end, when everything works, the gentlemen of creation fight over which of them came up with this brilliant idea first.

This has just happened now with Doctor B.'s private flat on the third floor of the center part of the main building in Königsfelden. Doctor B. is well regarded by Gloria. She likes his gallant and charming manner. She also likes the fact that he is not fixed on professional talk, that it is possible to discuss serious matters with him, such as opera and literature. Moreover, he is one of the few men who seems to enjoy the sight of her. She is aware of her womanly voluptuous curves. She likes to emphasize them with tight-fitting skirts, blouses and jumpers. She prides herself on being able to offer physically more than a flat ironing board figure with two sultanas for breasts. Moreover, Doctor B. does not seem to be offended by the circulating nasty rumours about her history, which have certainly been brought to his attention and which cause others to be arrogant towards her. No matter, Gloria always feels Doctor B.'s gaze spontaneously linger on her curves here and there with obvious pleasure. When Doctor B. took up his post as assistant doctor in Königsfelden almost ten years ago, coincidentally on the same day as Nurse Marga, the laboratory assistant, who later caught the always lively Doctor B. and became Mrs Doctor B., Gloria had still been working in the clinic in another capacity. When Doctor M. then was appointed head doctor of Königsfelden Clinic, he called her in as his secretary, as he doesn't give a damn about silly gossip and appreciates her professional qualities as a secretary.

The the administrator and the accountant of Königsfelden admonish for some time already, that the Health Department in Aarau objects, and rightly so, that two of the assistant doctors of Königsfelden clinic, Doctor P. and Doctor B., live outside the clinic in the village of Windisch. When it is clearly compulsory for the medical staff to live in the clinic compound. Now Head Doctor M. complains coincidentally, that two assistant doctors have just resigned and left the clinic at the same time and that it were extremly difficult to replace them. Now her, Gloria's, intuition is asked to point out, that the two former residents, who had left the clinic, had been living as unmarried men in quite luxurious rooms or even one- or two-room flats on the top floor in the main building of Königsfelden, close to each other. The one in spacious rooms equivalent to a two-room flat, with kitchen and bathroom and toilet, the other in a very spacious one-room flat, without kitchen, but with toilet. If these units, which are not exactly next to each other, were declared as one apartment for a family, it would be possible to bring one of the doctors living in the village of Windisch back to the clinic. For example, Doctor B. with his small family, who lives in a rented flat, that can he can easily leave at any time. Since Doctor P. had bought the house, in which he lives in Windisch, it would be less reasonable for him to move back to Königsfelden. If Doctor B. and his family move back to the clinic compound, it means, that Sister Marga, as Gloria still calls her, the present Mrs. Doctor B., whom Gloria likes very much, although they are fundamentally different, would be back in Königsfelden. Gloria would see and speak to her more often. Nurse Marga, although a daughter from a good family, practised a normal profession as a laboratory assistant until her marriage to Doctor B. and the birth of their first son. Moreover, she is not conceited at all. Even now that she is Mrs. Doctor B., she has not changed. Gloria also credits Nurse Marga for never having been dismissive towards her, like others who have moral reservations about her because of her history. Although fate has punished her, Gloria, severely for her misstep, which she has never regretted. Gloria is surprised that her boss, who usually looks after Doctor B. and his sister-in-law Gret, Mrs. Doctor B. or Nurse Marga, did not come up with this ingenious idea of using these vacated rooms as a flat for Doctor B. and his family.

Doctor B. and Nurse Marga are delighted with this apartment. They are not bothered by the fact that the two living units are devided by the huge entrance hall and the large ball room. Nurse Marga thinks it is perfect. In the living area with kitchen, bathroom, toilet and two rooms, they would set up their bedroom and the children's room, in the other area with the room of about one hundred square metres, the corridor and the toilet, the parlour with seating area and dining area. The rooms are huge, castle-like. From the aparment on the third floor of the building to his office, Doctor B. only needs to run down six flights of stairs, each with thirty steps each, past the head doctor's flat with the own entrance hall, endless corridors and the magnificent Green Hall, to the first floor, where his office is located. At mealtimes, he is upstairs with his family in no time.

From her box seat, when sitting at work at her desk in the antechamber of the head doctors office on the ground floor of the main building of the clinic, with her view through a window to the forecourt of the main building and to all people entering and leaving the house, Gloria unintentionally gets to know a lot about the habits and private everyday life of the people who work and who work and live in the house. Her boss is Head Doctor M.. He had been appointed as successor of Chief K., how the former head doctor had been called, wo had reached the age of retirement. Head Doctor M., and his family hat moved from the detached house behind the monastery church and near the stables of the clinic compound to the grand apartment of the respective head doctor, that occupies the entire second floor of the main building of the clinic. The little son of Head Doctor M. and his wife, Peider, soon started to get stuck in her office, when he explores the many corners of this most impressive building or wants to visit his father during work in his office. She loves it, when the primary school pupil Peider tells her about his life. Now that Doctor B. and Nurse Marga also live in the main building with their two small children, the toddler Bettina and little Rainer, who is called by everyone the Little One. His older cousin Peider, they say, had startet to call his little cousin, whom he had considered from the beginning on as his brother, affectionately the Little One. Head Doctor M. and his wife had adopted this name. Gloria also adopts it spontaneously. The Little One can already walk around independently in this huge building. He follows the footsteps of his big cousin Peider, whom he admires. So he, the Little One, ends up in her office as well. Although Doctor B. and Nurse Marga try to explain to little Rainer that she, Gloria, has to work. That he shouldn't disturb her. The Little One does not listen to his parents and turns up at Gloria's office at his whim. Gloria explains to his parents that the little boy doesn't disturb her at all. He sits down at the free desk in her office and then feels proud like an adult. When she gives him paper and crayons, he draws with fervour and doesn't disturb her at her work. Gloria, who is very fond of children, is happy that now that Peider is older and more independent and no longer comes to her office so often, she is one contact point for the Little One.

Another regular contact with the Little One arises in the context of her, Gloria's, professional activity.

In her younger years Gloria dreamt of becoming an opera singer. She had taken singing lessons. The urge to have a good breadwinning job and not to be financially dependent on her simple parents had put a spanner in her works. She had never been unhappy about it. Because of her singing and music training, it had occurred to her that she could set up and direct a choir with patients at the clinic. Head Doctor M. was enthusiastic, about this suggestion. With the help of the doctors and the nursing staff, she finds out which patients are willing and able to participate in the choir and selects the participants. The patients who are selected for the choir are enthusiastic, and Gloria has great fun with it. Choir rehearsals and performances take place in the clinic's ballroom, where the clinic's own and only piano stands. The ballroom is located between the two wings of Doctor B.s private family apartment. The Little One quickly checks when the weekly choir rehearsal is taking place. First he sneaks through his parents' appartment and various doors into the ballroom and hides behind the red velvet curtain of the theatre stage. She, Gloria, hears fumbling noises, suspects the Little One to be the source and asks him to come out of his hiding behind the theatre curtain. If he promised to be quiet as a mouse, he may listen without further ado and also stay in the ballroom.

The Little One confesses to Gloria, that he loves her, Gloria's, singing and her piano playing. He particularly enjoys being present and listening, when Gloria practices the piano and singing on her own outside of the choir rehearsals in the ballroom. So it happens that Gloria develops into a fixed point with limited family connection for Doctor B.'s und Nurse Marga's children. Now and then, when their parents are on a trip abroad she invites the Little One and his little sister to her home for meals. Then the Little One always asks for omelettes filled with minced meat. He loves this dish. They never had, he says and his little sister nodds with her head, this dish at home.

Nurse Marga likes to talk to Gloria about fashion. A dressmaker spends twice a year some days in the private apartments of Head Doctor M. and Doctor B. to adjust old dresses for the whole families and sometimes make a new dresses for Mrs. M. and Nurse Marga. Before the dressmaker arrives, Nurse Marga gets advice from her, Gloria, based on fashion magazines. Doctor B. in turn always finds an excuse to barge into her, Gloria's, office. Then he pretends to apologize for the disturbance, but expects her, Gloria, to invite him into her office for a chat. Recently, he gave up smoking cigarettes. He declares that, in order to reduce his smoking, he will only have a cigars now and then. But if she offers him one of her Mary Long cigarettes, he never says no. Pretending, out of politeness. She knows that if he feels like a cigarette, he will barge into her office. Then they talk about new publications in the field of literature and about the latest opera performances in Zürich. Topics that are of burning interest to both of them. As a formality, Doctor B. keeps apologizing to Gloria that his two children bother her so often. Gloria reassures Doctor B., she loved children, and they are so well-behaved that they never disturb her at work. Especially the Little One is so sensitive and creative.

"Nice of you to say that, Miss G.," Doctor B. interjects between two puffs from his Mary Long cigarette, "but he also should learn to fight with other boys instead of always running away, when other boys face him!"

The Little One loves to draw. As a little boy, he drew clumsily and out of a childish wild imagination. As he grows older, he develops a distinct skill in drawing and she, Gloria, sees that he has a real talent for drawing. He draws mostly women. Beautiful women. She criticizes his drawings and suggests corrections, when the proportions of the figures are not right. Guides him to study the figures in fashion magazines, that she hands him. In order to then see from the photographs how he could perfect his drawings. The little boy immerses himself in the magazines. Then he gets started.

From his imagination, he draws women in the most beautiful evening gowns. With so much skill and sense of form that she is totally enthralled.

"Why do you only draw women and not men", she asks him.

The little boy looks at Gloria with a serious look and then begins his lecture.

"Women are beautiful, Miss G.!"

"Men aren't?"

The Little One pauses. He looks at Gloria as if she had said the most ridiculous thing. Then he has a fit of laughter. So that Gloria wonders if he will ever stop laughing again. This reaction of him touches her strangely. He often complains bitterly that his parents demand an awful lot more of him than they do of his little sister. He is scolded for doing or not doing a certain thing, while the parents smile at his little sister for doing or not doing the same thing and do not reprimand her. She, Gloria, also sees, how Doctor B., as a proud father, spoils his little girl, as he calls it, to the hilt and looks at her with a mild smile, while he demands of his offspring, as he calls his son, a clearly masculine and snappy demeanour and defensiveness. The Little One, who is not a wild boy, makes a face when his father reprimands him and does not seem to be impressed any further.

After work, before she goes home, Gloria packs the Little One's latest drawings and proudly shows them to Nurse Marga, Mrs. M. and other women. Doctor B. also bursts into this group. He overhears the women having fun and enjoying the drawings. Until one of the women exclaims delightedly, "The Little One will certainly become a fashion designer one day, a second Dior!" Gloria notices how Doctor B.'s facial expression at these words shows pure horror. Instead of rejoicing in his boy's creativity, he apparently dismisses it as feminine posturing. When he notices how she, Gloria, looks at him, he grimaces and shakes his head. A son with such talents seems to be a difficult toad to swallow for the educated and so charming Doctor B. as a father. Doctor B. makes no secret of the fact that he thoroughly admires the Little One's cousin, Peider, who is seven years older than him, a jock and in a way a swashbuckler. Doctor B. seems to regret deeply, that his son does not follow the example of Peider, whom the Little One admires so much and with whom he always hangs out.

Gloria can observe the Little One's growing up from an outside perspective and gets to see things that interest her and that she herself was never able to experience with her own son, Butzli.

The Little One now is a proud kindergartener. He is allowed to leave the Königsfelden park unaccompanied. Carefully, looking left and right, crossing the busy Zürcherstrasse. Enter the village and walk along the familiar path to the house where the kindergarten is located. One fine day, Doctor B. once again seeks out her, Gloria, in her office. To her astonishment, this time Doctor B. is not as buoyant and ironically mischievous as usual. Contrary to his habit, he does not wait until she asks him to take a seat. Without being asked, he sits down on the unused desk in her office. As if mechanically, he takes the Mary Long cigarette she immediately offers him and stares into the floor in front of him.

"Miss G., you have known me for years, and I value you highly as a confidant. How should I behave? I don't know. Rainer titled me 'Father, you're stupid!' in front of the father of a kindergarten classmate, a simple labourer, as he, Doctor B., had tried to clarify it for him, his son, that he shouldn't be so dreamy and not even know where he lived and what his surname was. The son stamped defiantly on the floor. The simple worker had to suppress a laugh. The doctor being called stupid by his son! How do I stand as a father in front of this simple man!"

Gloria already knew part of the background to this story from the day before. In the later afternoon yesterday, Nurse Marga had stormed flustered into Gloria's office and asked, if the Little One was here with her. He should have been back from kindergarten well over an hour ago. Gloria tries to calm the flabbergasted Nurse Marga. The Little One would surely show up soon. Later, Gloria had glanced out of the window and seen Doctor B. hurry out of the main building and walk past the roundabout with the Roman fountain towards the village. She assumes that Doctor B. had been asked by Nurse Marga to go to the kindergarten and the village, searching for his son. Head Doctor M. also already knew about the disappearance of the Little One. But he is sure that the Little One will turn up again. Even small children need their space and usually reappear as soon as they are hungry. Some time later, again looking out of her office window, Gloria is relieved to see father and son trudging in unison past the roundabout towards the main building. That is, father and son are walking side by side. Both stare at the ground as they walk, and she, Gloria, suspects that there is not a good atmosphere between them. So now Gloria has the explanation why the air had been thick yesterday, but she still doesn't know what really had happened. She is sure that the Little One will come to her soon and tell her more. She doesn't want to ask Doctor B. about the circumstances. She consoles him by saying that children give free rein to their feelings and sometimes say something in anger that is forgotten again shortly afterwards.

"You are right, Miss G.. My wife has already said that I shouldn't be so hard on Rainer and shouldn't take his moods too seriously. Thank you for the cigarette. It did me good to talk to you", Doctor B. says. He stubs out the cigarette in the ashtray and shuffles off.

Shortly afterwards, after a gentle knock, the Little One pokes his head through the crack of the slightly opened office door, then pushes himself all the way into Gloria's office, plants himself proudly in front of her, looks at her and asks, beaming, "Look, Miss G., do you see anything?".

Gloria smiles at the boy. She examines him from head to toe and shakes her head to indicate, that she sees nothing out of the ordinary.

"The right shoe is on the right foot. Without Hedeli or the kindergarten aunt helping me. And I also tied the shoe laces myself. The loops aren't quite as nice as when Hedeli ..."

Gloria pretends to stare in wonder at the Little One's feet stuck in the shoes and nods in enthusiastic recognition.

"And what did you manage to do yesterday, that you didn't get home on time after kindergarten?"

"Nothing. Hedeli has such beautiful eyes. And she always tells me which shoe belongs on which foot. And then she also ties my shoes with the laces. But I've already told you that, Miss G.. After kindergarten, I told her that she ties my shoelaces into such beautiful loops. And suddenly Hedeli says. I live there, if you want, come in. Miss G., you've never seen anything like it. Such a small kitchen. Kitchen table. Corner bench. And Hedeli's father, such a posture," the Little One puffs himself up and sticks out his chest. "And you know what, he was only wearing a undershirt, without sleeves, he had many, many hairs on his arms that stood up like that. And Hedeli's father talked to me as if I were grown up. And Hedeli's mummy gave me cider. And we ate bread with butter and sugar."

"Aha, and then you didn't know where you lived and what your name was!"

"That's what Father told you! Hedeli's father said, it's high time now. You have to go home, otherwise your parents will be afraid. Where do you live, and what is your surname? I couldn't think of it. Hedeli's father took me by the hand and walked with me through the whole village. He always asked me, do you live there or there? And then we met Father. He told me to stop dreaming. How can I stop dreaming when it's dreaming out of me. Children are stupid, okay. But they are not grown up yet either. Father orders, stop dreaming. It's stupid. I can't stop dreaming."

Gloria is amused at how she becomes the wailing wall of father and son in their shadow fights. She is not particularly surprised that the two clash so often. The snappy father, who sees in Peider's example how he wants his son to be. And the son who is dreamy and unflinchingly goes his own way. But the Little One is not only at the mercy of his father's ideas. His mother, Nurse Marga, also has her own ideas. The Little One now attends primary school. When Gloria goes to work, she meets the pupils walking towards the school on the village street. Among them is the Little One. He is very different from the children in the village. He and Martin, another boy from Königsfelden, the son of a colleague of Doctor B., clearly do not belong to the cliques of the boys from the village. The Little One still shows up regularly in Gloria's office.

"Do you know, Miss G., what the boys from the village call you?"

"The boys from the village know me and have a name for me?"

"Because you cross us every day, right on time, when we go to school. The boys from the village call you 'the eight-o'clock-woman'. Because it's always just before eight when we meet you."

"Funny. You're wearing really nice trousers and a really smart jumper again."

"Before me, Peider had to wear these trousers until they got too small for him and Miss H., the dressmaker, altered them for me, so that I wouldn't, as Mum says, grow out of them again straight away. Therefore, always much too big and baggy. Like a clown. Mummy wants me to wear them. It's okay. I'd rather have dark blue, really tight Manchester trousers with rips in them like all the boys in the village, but Mummy says, be proud that you get special clothes and don't have to walk around like everyone else! And then the red jumper. Mummy loves to knit. Then she knitted me red cap as well to match the jumper. Here. I always take it off when I'm out of the house and Mummy doesn't see me anymore. The first time I had to wear this red jumper and the red cap, the boys from the village mocked me as Little Red Riding Hood. And if the boys from the village don't laugh at me because of my clothes, then it's because I'm a total loser at sport, scared of every ball that comes my way. Or because I have no muscles, am a bone-head, a weakling. Also, because I got a day off school, so that I could fly with Mummy to Stuttgart to visit my godmother Ilse. Ah. But when I say to my schoolmates, "Do you want to see skulls", then all the boys who usually pester me, are suddenly nice and say, "Oh yes!" Then they all come along, terrified to enter the monastery park because they are afraid of the patients and their parents have forbidden them to go near the Monastery. But the boys are tempted to do the forbidden and see real skulls. The loud-mouthed ones suddenly become meek and quite okay. Then I lead them into the monastery church. They follow me hesitantly, suspiciously. Then I let them see the skulls of the fallen Austrian knights at the Battle of Sempach on the catafalque. Then the boys are amazed. Their eyes almost fall out of their heads. Then they don't mock me. Then they don't care, that the weakling is their leader for a few hours. And two boys never join in when the others beat me up. These two boys are really nice. I'm even allowed to go on bike trips with the parents of one of them because my parents don't ride bikes with us."

"Did you tell Mummy that you wanted different clothes? Did you tell Father that the boys in the village were mocking you?"

"Yes. But Mummy says I'm a spoilt boy. And should be content. I can't do anything right for Father anyway, and if I say I'm being made fun of, he'll make fun of me too. I'm not allowed to read Mickey Mouse magazines, Biggels or Karl May books, like the boys of the village. But if I say everyone else can, he says mockingly, are you 'everyone else'? Vox populi vox Rindvieh (The voice of the people, the

144

voice of the cattle). He thinks I don't know what that means. But I do. Peider told me. In return, Father gives me 'Soll und Haben' by Gustav Freytag, 'Der kleine Lord' by Frances Hodgson Burnett and 'Der Trompeter von Säckingen' by Viktor von Scheffel. That's all right. Father is always so strict and scolds me. For Christmas, he gave me a Black Forest clock that I could put together myself. At the same time I got a book from my godfather and started looking at it. Then Father started to put the clock together. I was not allowed to help. He said, I was too clumsy. And that I was a spoiled boy who couldn't even enjoy putting together a Black Forest clock. But I just wanted to look at the book first and then ... And then Father gave me the Poets Quartet card play. On each of the playing cards is a portrait of a poet with his name and the three other poets belonging to the same category. I like the name Walter von der Vogelweide and I know the poem 'Dû bist mîn, ich bin dîn, des solt dû gewis sîn, dû bist beslozzen, in mînem herzen, verlorn ist das sluzzelîn: dû muost ouch immêr darinne sîn' (love poem by a minstrel around the year 1200 in ancient German) by heart. I particularly like the portraits of Heinrich Heine, Novalis and Josef von Eichendorff. You're amazed, aren't you? It's okay with all the books I get. I can talk yout everything to my godfather, on the other hand. And my godfather tells me that the boys in the village envy me because I'm so clever at school. I shouldn't let myself be impressed. If I had a different father, like Peider, who has my godfather as his father, then I would be different too. But my godfather tells me, I should stay the way I am."

Gloria knows that the Little One's godfather is her boss, Head Doctor M.. She is surprised that in these circumstances, which seem so idyllic on the outside, there is something wrong. Although she has the trust of all those close to the Little One, she wants to avoid getting actively involved and share her own thoughts with Doctor B. and Nurse Marga. Finally, the Little One stubbornly goes his own way. Doesn't seem to really suffer from the shadow fights. He seems to bear his tense relationship with his father and his emotional distance from his mother with composure. He knows how to help himself and remains a lovable, cheerful, open-minded and imaginative boy despite everything. And he confides many things in her, Gloria.

The father definitely wants that his son be guided to follow the example of his cousin Peider. Peider is an enthusiastic Boy Scout. The son must become a real boy. The Little One confesses to Gloria that he refused at first. But then Godfather advised him not to refuse straight away, but to go there first and see, whether he liked it there, with the little wolves, the little Boy Scouts, or not. Gloria learns that the Little One is accepted into a pack of wolves and is baptized with the scout name Beetle. The Little One is embarrassed by this name. His fellow wolves now call him Beetle all the time. Even at school and in the village. Classmates who overhear this Boy Scout name, laugh at him.

Then happens something, that the Little One keeps from her, Gloria. But Gloria learns about, in fragments, from his little sister Bettina and Nurse Marga.

Little Bettina tells Gloria the latest development in the father-son relationship.
"Father yelled at Raini. 'You're a liar'. Raini yells back, ‚I didn't lie'. Father and Raini run after each other around the dining table. Father catches Raini. Pulls down his

trousers, puts him over his knee and beats Raini's naked buttocks like crazy. In the process, Father gets a bright red head and dances all around as he punches. So I'm afraid he'll smash Raini's head against an edge of the dining room buffet."

Gloria learns the backstory from Nurse Marga. Her Hansel had a man from the village in outpatient treatment because his son had psychological difficulties. Hansel then suggested to the man that the son should join the Boy Scouts in order to socialize with other children. Hansel then asked Rainer if another boy could be accepted into his pack of wolves. Rainer told him that the leader, Darsie, had said a few days ago, that their pack was already too big and that no new wolves could be accepted. Therefore, there were a moratorium on admissions and no wolve should ask for other boys to be admitted in their pack. Hansel, that's just the way it is, always mistrusts his son's statements. He called Darsie and asked nicely if another boy could be admitted to the group. Darsie explained to the doctor that it was of course possible.

"You know the rest of the story, Miss G.. It did not help in any way to ease the relationship between father and son. I myself called Darsie later to ask, whether she had actually declared before to the boys, that there was a ban on admissions to her pack of wolves. She told me, that she had done so. But she could not say no to Doctor B.. He hadn't asked her about the admission freeze, and she had no reason to talk about it herself," says Nurse Marga and puffs out loudly. "I don't get involved any more. What I would say to Hansel or Rainer adds new fuel to the fire. Those two have to get along on their own, don't they, Miss G.?! The boy is difficult. The other day, he totally embarrassed me. We were

147

walking in town. On the pavement on the other side of the street, Signora C., the mistress of factory owner K., approaches in our direction. You know, 'that certain Signora C.,' who wears such outrageously tight clothes that ,when she walks on her high-heeled shoes, everything of her body wobbles in front and behind. I notice how Rainer stares at Signora C., with such eyes and with his mouth open in amazement. I admonish him, not to stare at this person. He has the cheek to ask me, why we don't greet her. She were so beautiful and stunning. I have to control myself not to smack him right away. I say we don't greet her. We treat her like air. When Signora C. has long since passed our height, I become aware of my son, my son turning around and staring in amazement at Signora C.'s wiggling bottom. My hand slipped. But how does my son react?! He laughs at me. And when I tell my Hansel this outrageous story, he has nothing better to say than, 'you learn to cook on old pans'. And this about his eleven-year-old son! My dear Hansel is not without faults and the Little One, well, the apple doesn't fall far from the tree. God knows I have more important things to do than to flutter around as an angel of peace and, when the roosters are fighting in addition .... My Hansel works so much and has so many things to do in his spare time, that there is little time left for arguing. And you will hardly believe it, Miss G., when we are in Oberrohrdorf with Nänne and Vatter, my two men play brilliantly on a harmonious father-son relationship. Sometimes I envy you, Miss G., that you don't have to deal with husband and son every day."

Gloria is silent. She sees it differently. If the father of her son had not been married, and she had fallen into disrepute because of the pregnancy, if the cute son, Butzli, had not fallen victim to a traffic accident ...

In the Head Doctor M.'s private household, an au pair girl from Lyon, Yvette, has arrived. The Little One seems to have taken a fancy to Yvette, who is only four years older than him and extremely pretty and likeable. He now spends the time he used to spend with her, Gloria, in her office, hanging out with Yvette in the the head doctor's appartment, in the kitchen or wherever Yvette is supposed to do housework. Gloria is amazed at how he picks up bits of French in no time and is soon able to converse in French.

"How did you manage that," Gloria asks him.

"C'est simple comme bonjour," the Little One replies. Yvette and I listen to French chansons by Juliette Gréco. And Yvette always buys Jours de France and Paris Match, and we read the magazines together. If I don't know French, it doesn't work."

The Little One is getting older. Twelve years old. Now he attends no longer the Primary School in the village Windisch, but the District School in the small town Brugg. His visits to Gloria become more sparse. To Gloria's delight, the relationship remains. Whenever Doctor B. and Nurse Marga are on holiday without the children, she invites the now grown-up Litte One and his sister Bettina to her home for omelettes filled with minced meat. The children and also she, Gloria, enjoy being together.

8.

Doctor of Philology Heinrich R., a German and history teacher at the Brugg District School, has been known as 'Grey Heinrich' among his closest friends and family for since he can remember. He got this designation after Heinrich's older brother, exasperated by some behaviour of his younger brother, had sighed loudly in front of the whole family, "Heinrich, mir graut vor dir" (quoting Gretchen from Goethe's Faust: ,Heinrich, I am dreading you'. In German dreadig is spelled and sounds like the colour grey!). His father said with a grin, "yes, yes, our Grey Heinrich!" This name from then on stuck to him and spread to most of his acquaintances. Even his pupils at school and his fellow teachers have got wind of this name. Secretly, he is proud to be so important to his pupils, that they give him an epithet behind his back, but still, when adressing him directly, call him then decently Dr. R..

Grey Heinrich gives his Vera a little kiss as a farewell for the day. He leaves to get on his bicycle outside the house. Vera looks after him. Shouts in horror, "But you're not going to school dressed like that!"

"Yes I am, I'm going to school like this."

"Heinrich, Heinrich!"

"All that's missing now is that you compete your words with ,I am dreading you'!", and Heinrich is gone.

Vera watches him go. By now, she is smiling. Somehow, she likes his impertinent coquetry.

Among friends, Vera and Heinrich had recently been out for a walk, making a pilgrimage to the garden restaurant Habsburg. Heinrich and his friends noticed that the women had lagged behind a bit and were suddenly giggling horribly about something. When asked what was so funny, they had cried out in unison, giggling, "nothing, nothing, nothing".

Later, Vera confessed to Grey Heinrich that the women's gaze had involuntarily fallen on the men's bottoms as they walked behind them. The women then gave out marks for the bottoms. His, Heinrich's, bottom had received the highest mark from all the women.

"You mocked my ass!!! Shame and disgrace on you. It's not my fault that ..."

"In those light beige linen trousers, which fit so perfectly, that is to say, tightly, plus the light white short-sleeved shirt, which also fits like a glove, then as you walk, your fortunately so round and shapely buttocks muscles play, that it is a joy and totally delightful to stare at them, one can hardly take one's eyes off them. It had made us giggle."

"You and your filthy thoughts," murmurs Grey Heinrich in an acted threatening tone, lunging at Vera to give her a burning kiss and to - let's not this elaborate any further. And now in just this outfit, the white short-sleeved shirt and the beige, light linen trousers, that are rather new, Grey Heinrich has just swung himself onto his bicycle to ride for the first time in this outfit to class at the district school.

Since the incident during the walk with his friends and the subsequent confession of his Vera, the white short-sleeved shirt and the beige linen trousers are Grey Heinrich's preferred summer clothes. He feels comfortable in them, and the awareness of possessing an attractive body, of which he has nothing to be ashamed of, fills him with satisfaction. The other day he had dressed the same way for a meeting in the Sternen Club. In the Sternen Club various men interested in literature meet at regular intervals in the Restaurant Sternen (star) near the medivial Black Tower in the old town of Brugg to discuss literature, especially newly published novels. In the Sternen Club Grey Heinrich meets a certain Doctor B., a German by birth, who has been working in the Psychiatric Clinic Königsfelden, the so called Monastery, as a senior physician and psychiatrist for decades and who has a reputation for impeccable humanistic education and the greatest interest in literature. Conversations with this Doctor B., who is so very different from the Brugger men, are highly stimulating and a real pleasure. His knowledge of literature and his connecting the literary works with the lives and personalities of the writers and thinkers is outstanding. And yet, Grey Heinrich wonders why he never really warms up to this Doctor B.. Why he remains distant, even though they get on very well. He attributes this to their different backgrounds. With such knowledge, Doctor B. must come from an upper class in Germany, which simply does not exist in the small town of Brugg. At a recent meeting of the Sternen Club, where Grey Heinrich, considering the summer temperature, had taken the liberty of appearing without a jacket and in his latest favourite outfit, he meets Doctor B. already on the way to the Restaurant Sternen on the main street in Brugg.

Grey Heinrich is pleased and approaches Doctor B.. Doctor B. is also visibly pleased. Before a casual and exciting conversation ensues, Grey Heinrich notices how Doctor B. casually, hardly noticeably, examines him, Grey Heinrich, from head to toe and spontaneously, for a fraction of a second, contorts his face into an indignant expression. The perception of this random, fleeting, barely noticeable glance in Doctor B.'s face triggers a click in Grey Heinrich's head, that generates a jumble of thoughts that secretly accompanies Grey Heinrich along the way throughout the evening. He and this Doctor B. are worlds apart.

At their first meeting and at the first getting to know each other, Doctor B. had visibly exclaimed with great joy, "Oh, you are a doctor of philology!" Grey Heinrich is totally thrilled, that Doctor B. values his formation, about which here nobody ever cares. This casual remark by Doctor B. touches him. He notices as well, that Doctor B. is a most refined person, pays attention to correct and good clothing. Never overdressed, but always recognizable as a well-dressed man. His male uniform fits perfectly. And is well tailored. Always, even in high summer, a perfectly fitting jacket that is not too body-hugging. Now in summer, made of white linen. Grey Heinrich reflects that Doctor B. could not possibly have obtained such a garment in a Brugger men's clothing shop. That he very probably buys his clothes in Zurich or has them tailored there. Clothes make the man and, when observed sharply and not just superficially, reveal the origin, class and self-image of the person wearing them.

Grey Heinrich perceives Doctor B.'s appearance as inconspicuously noble - he can't call it anything else - unobtrusive, rather distant, distracting from the body, referring to the mind. Grey Heinrich is amused by the thoughts a brief glance is capable of generating. And just on this day when he had swung himself onto his bicycle in his breezy summer clothes to ride to school, it occurs to him, that in the new class assigned to him as class teacher, one pupil bears the surname B., like Doktor B.. Since this name is clearly German and does not occur elsewhere in the area, the boy must be Doctor B.'s son. He must secretly observe this boy. As unnoticed as possible. This constellation, that he knows a father from a club and has the son as a pupil, lends itself to the study of social conditions. Grey Heinrich is terribly curious to find out, how son and father resemble each other.

In the school lesson, Grey Heinrich distributes the corrected school essays he had the pupils write on the subject 'How to learn to lie'. Grey Heinrich stands next to his desk. Takes the pile of essays from his briefcase lying on the desk. Reads down the names of the pupils one by one. Makes them come out of the school desks to him to hand them back their work. For the first time, he consciously notices Rainer B.. A handsome, somewhat inconspicuous boy of fine build, with a cheerful face and a vivid look. And it is precisely this look that Grey Heinrich notices in a fraction of a second, how it obviously slides down his, Grey Heinrich's, body. Briefly sticks at the level of the buttocks. Thereby changing the boy's facial expression for a fraction of a second to joyful amazement. Quckily afterwards the boy's eyes are directed to his, Grey Heinrich's, face, now with a serious facial expression. Something clicks in Grey Heinrich's brain. Worlds separate the father from the son. Unlike the father, the son seems to react joyfully to random sensory stimuli, as bodies can give. Grey Heinrich basks in the idea of having a well-formed body. He enjoys appreciative glances, wherever they may come from. He gives young B. back his essay.

Essay No. 3 of May 29, 1957
How to learn to lie

Lying, oh, that cannot be learned. A lie often slips out of one's mouth without one's wanting it to. You don't want to bring out the truth. I was still in the first grade when I once was ordered by my school teacher as a punishment for too many spelling mistakes in an essay to go to school already at 7 o'clock instead of, as usually at 8 o'clock. I went all the way from home to the stables of the clinic and hided. There I waited until five minutes before 8 o'cock and then went to class at the same hour as the other pupils. After school, I went home as if nothing unusual had happened. Did you go to school at 7 o'clock, my father asked me with a harsh voice. I said yes. He repeated his question several times. I lied three times. Then there was trouble because he had heard from my teacher, that I had not been at school at 7 o'cock. He punished me. If only one could unlearn to lie.

After the end of the German lesson, Grey Heinrich dismisses the boys. He asks young B. to stay for a moment and hand him back his essay. He wants to briefly skim over his essay again. He had a vague, but no longer concrete recollection, that the boy mentioned his father in some form in his essay. While he briefly skims the essay again and sees that in the son's essay the father appears as a rebuking authority, the boy steps boredly from one foot to the other and waits. Grey Heinrich thanks him. Gives him back his essay. Dismisses him with the words, "You write with a lot of imagination. As soon as your spelling improves, you'll get top marks."

Young B.'s next essay again shows a lush imagination and a gift for storytelling.

<u>Essay No. 5 from June 26, 1957</u>
<u>Ghosts</u>
A young man who lived in a big city and worked as a doctor found a letter in the morning on the treshold of his apartment. He opened the envelope with a crackle and deciphered what was written. He understood from it, that he was expected at the big bridge at midnight to negotiate something important. The signature was missing. It was a mystery to him how the letter got here. But the man went to the bridge. It was quiet there, but from a distance, he suddenly heard footsteps, and the man felt uneasy. Without him noticing, a ghost in a red coat crept up and asked him: "You are a doctor, aren't you? Follow me!" He startled and stammered: "Yes" and followed the Redcoat into a cellar. The Redcoat told him, "My sister has died, and now we want to embalm her, we want to give her father her head, so you must behead her." Then the Redcoat disappeared. The man took his knife and began to cut. As he was about to take the sharper knife, the dead woman opened her

eyes once more and tried to sit up, but she fell back again. He quickly cut off her head completely and looked for the exit and disappeared. At home, he realized that he had left the knife behind. The next day, a neighbour told him that the mayor's daughter, who was to be married today, had been murdered. The man got a fright. Soon, the police came with his knife and asked him if the knife belonged to him. He answered in the affirmative. He came to court. He kept saying, "I have been seduced", but the court decided to cut off one of his hands. He never saw the Redcoat again.

Dealing with this story spontaneously awakens the hobby psychologist in Grey Heinrich. It cannot be a coincidence that young B. makes a doctor the protagonist in the invented story. This doctor chops off the head of a woman, the anima, on the orders of a mysterious stranger and is punished by having one of his hands, his best tool, chopped off in turn, while the driving force remains missing.

The fact that Doctor B.'s son is a disciple of Grey Heinrich is sometimes briefly fiddled with by the two of them in passing at meetings of the Sternen Club. Doctor B. laughingly asks Grey Heinrich if his offspring is doing anything right in German class or is also throwing tantrums like he does at home, so that one feels winded and sore. Grey Heinrich laughs. At school, he is rather reserved or shy, but a very pleasant, bright pupil who participates well in class.

Grey Heinrich does not mention the recent incident with the Redcoat essay to Doctor B..

One day the gym teacher turned up in Grey Heinrich's classroom during a break, quite concerned and embarrassed.

"You know, I'm terribly embarrassed. I embarrassed one of your pupils during a lesson. He laughed happily with me, but I don't know, if I didn't go too far. In the last lesson the boys had asked me, what I had had to do to be so athletic and have such muscles. To show them vividly that it's all just training and stamina, I told them that when I was a boy I used to be a lanky little lad, like him, B.. All the boys looked from me to B. and back in disbelief. Then they burst out laughing. That couldn't be! A loser like B. could never become a sensible sportsman! As I said, B. laughed along. When I wanted to talk to him after the lesson and apologize, he was already gone. And now I don't want to talk to him about it again, but I want to confess my mistake to you as B's class teacher. Perhaps you can tell him, how sorry I feel."

Grey Heinrich holds B. back after a school lesson on any pretext, chats with him somehow, and then casually confesses to him, what he had been told about this ominous gym lesson. B. laughs. Waves it off. He were a loser in sports. Everyone knew that. But teacher W., the gym teacher, were really great. He never forced him to do exercises on the high bar or the pole in gym class, which he is terrified of. Teacher W. were allowed to unabashedly call him a bottle in front of everyone. It were an open secret that he was a loser in gymnastics and especially in the ball games that are so popular with the wild boys at school.

A short time later, gymnastics teacher W. has a fatal car accident during his military service and dies. Peider

M. and Helmut S., both now university students, widely known from the Boy Scouts and sports clubs, are temporarily appointed as substitute gym teachers. Both are extremely attractive young men. Idols of the male youth of the area. At the same time, idols of the female youth of the area. When it becomes known at school that idolized Peider is B.'s cousin, and that B. also knows Peider's friend Helmut very well, B.'s prestige rises enormously. Everyone wants to get in good terms with him in order to draw Peider and Helmut's attention to them. Even in the class parliament, which Grey Heinrich initiates in this school class of which he is the class teacher, B. takes on the role he has always played in the community of pupils, as he witnesses with amusement. B. is not a ringleader. He never speaks out. Observes from the sidelines in silence. As if he is not part of the group. Only dares to make a critical comment now and then. Which is always well-founded and for which the others show him respect.

Essay No. 16 of March 6, 1959
Short joy
"Latin, whew, vocabulary vocabulary and vocabulary again; learning, learning and learning, bad marks, quarrelling with father, oh, the misfortunes of Latin are indescribable." That's how I rage on Saturday. Why? A bad grade. Consequences? The father scolds, the mother scolds. After a few days, the father says, "Oh, Latin is a very beautiful language, isn't it?" "Oh, yes!" I have to reply.
In the middle of the rain, a bit of sunshine. In the middle of bad notes, a good one. Afterwards, I go to work with such zeal. Then

it's: Work, work, make more such good notes. I work. The father says, "Now the mark in the report card should be much better." I say nothing!!!!

I already know the consequences of a good mark: the next five papers the hand doesn't want to do properly, it doesn't want to obey me and writes what it wants; during the next five papers I rage so much that no good mark can come about. Then soon comes another good period. A short period of joy, but it always changes.

Now that Grey Heinrich knows father and son, he follows with great amusement how the father appears in the son's essays. As much as the B. family appears to the public as an idyllic community. For instance on the for most middle-class families customary Sunday afternoon walks along the Aare from Brugg to Schinznach Bad. Grey Heinrich can now and then by chance see, how the B. family sits idyllically together round a table at the ‚thé dansant' (tea and danse in the afteroon) in the noble spa hotel with drinks and cake. Even then is clear, that the son philanders with the sister and sometimes the mother, but left the father out. Together with the situations taken from the son's essays, Grey Heinrich can imagine that at home at B.'s it is sometimes like a wooden heaven between father and son, that there are fights, in the bright light or also in the shadows.

Grey Heinrich doesn't often inquire, but if he can't think of anything better to do, how the pupils of his class are doing in class with other teachers. This time he asks the doyen of the teaching staff at the Brugg District School,

Dr. F.. Who is generally nicknamed Sperber (Sparrowhawk), because of his sparrowhawk look through his pince-nez. Sperber teaches French and Latin. When the subject of young B. came up, Sperber begins to talk animatedly.

"Colleague R., have you also noticed how creative and imaginative young B. is? On the margins of his textbooks and in his notebooks, he scribbles little sketches that are so skilful. One is amazed. In Latin, he is a failure. Doesn't do anything and doesn't care about bad marks. In French, on the other hand, he is a killer. When I ask him how it is that he speaks such wonderful French and can formulate imaginative sentences, he looks at me shaking his head. At his aunt and uncle's, who lived in the same house as he did, there was an au pair girl from Lyon, Yvette, in addition to the maid. When he speaks to her, it had to be in French because she does not yet speak German. In addition, Yvette buys the magazine Paris-Match every week. If he wouldn't know French, he couldnt read the magazine. He also received an old radio set from his older cousin Peider and, after a long search, found a French station on which the song Milord by Edith Piaf is broadcast over and over again. In the meantime, he knew the lyrics by heart. The boy, although dreamy and not very integrated into the class, is a phenomenon. But unfortunately, I made a mistake lately. My wife and I know Doctor B. and his wife, young B.'s parents, since we attended a Bible group together years ago. The other day I met Doctor B. and his wife on the street. Congratulated them on their successful son. I mentioned that the boy was so imaginative that further education at a school of arts and crafts would be suitable for him. First Doctor B., then his wife, burst out laughing. Between laughs, Doctor B. pressed out, that this was probably to be understood as a joke. In his family, all the men graduated from college and went on to get their doctorates at university!"

For Grey Heinrich, the picture of the relationship between father and son B. rounds off. The side blow that the son gives the father also fits into this picture by accusing him of acting like a do-gooder.

Essay No. 7 of October 29, 1959
I am trading.*

I'm in a very bad way with my money now, I was on holiday and needed over ten francs, all my savings. Now I have to save and run as many errands as possible so that I can take my snapped photos to be developed.

Income: My salary per week is fifty cents, paid by my mother.

Secondary income: My father prides himself of being generous : I take his letters to the postbox at the railway station, fetch newspapers from the kiosk at the railway station. Every single course is remunerated with ten or twenty cents. Trade: My cousin needs money to go to the cinema, I lend him a franc, on which I charge ten percent interest, sometimes I have to fight for the interest. But the main source of income is my grandmother. She eats with us every other day, then I fetch her when mother has cooked. Then grandmother asks me every time if I am in need of money, in the past I said yes and got fifty cents, now I say yes every third time, but then I get three or five francs.

Expenses: Very big! For birthdays and for photography.

These are my expenses and income, whereby the expenses are usually bigger than the income.

*My finances

Grey Heinrich approaches Doctor B. in the offside at a Sternen Club meeting about his son. He says that the boy is exceptionally good in written work when he really tries hard. What he mostly does. Then he is above average. Which indicates a very good intelligence. At these words, Doctor B.'s facial features relax. He throws in a smirk with an ironic tone, "how could it be otherwise with such a mother, and such a father", and then laughs.

"But as soon as Rainer is called upon and has to hold his own orally, in oral exams, he begins to sweat, he blushes, he stutters. Plainly, he is blocked. As a layman in psychological matters, I wonder if there is a case of test anxiety."

"Oh, Dr. R., don't fall for this cunning fellow. He's playing you. To get sympathy. No one in my family has ever suffered from test anxiety."

Essay No. 8 of November 26, 1959

About my father's profession (teacher's correction in red: and my future).

My father is a doctor, like my grandfather, and he wants me to take up this profession too. However, I don't like it. And whether I would be clever enough for it?

My father has to deal with the patients of the clinic all day long, and on certain afternoons he visits homes for handicaped people and prisons. He has to extort or elicit facts from people and then write them up into expert reports. Since I am also far too volatile, I could not write down all the details of such reports, which are sometimes very important. My father sits in the office all day, so to speak, which doesn't suit me either. One could get used to this, but I don't like the whole thing. But I will complete the fourth grade of the District School if possible, and what happens afterwards will be clear when I know exactly what I want to become. My father works eight hours a day and in the evenings as well. As far as I know, he has to work every third Saturday afternoon and Sunday. So, he has to work a lot. He has four weeks of holiday per year. The father is employed by the state. He also has to give school lessons to young male and female nurses and train them.

Grey Heinrich grins when reading this essay by young B.. The sly little fellow does not limit himself to describing his father's profession, but clearly states that he does not want to become, what the father is. There seems to be open warfare between father and son B., a 'drôle de guerre'. Two stubborn goats who cannot refrain from repeatedly going at each other horns first. The creative and imaginative son does not want to be imprisoned in the stiff and implacable world of his father. The madness of how bitter relationship fights play out in the shadow of the seemingly idyllic family!

Grey Heinrich is surprised that young B. fails the exam to enter the Cantonal High School in Aarau. Then he is successful in the admission exam in a private gymnasium in Zurich.

"Typical my aristocratic son of a proletarian father," Doctor B. complains to Grey Heinrich occasionally. "A public gymnasium didn't do it for him. It must be a private gymnasium. And an expensive and noble one at that. And my wife, his aunt Bertie, Mrs. M., and his godfather Head Doctor M., support his wishes, as his cousin Peider had also attended the same gymnasium in Zurich!"

9.

The son is happy to follow in the footsteps of his cousin Peider, whom he admires, and attend the same gymnasium in Zurich, that he had attended. He is eager to learn new things. A new phase of life begins. He has also surpassed his father in height. Not by much, but still by two or three centimetres. He looks at this man who is his father. Something repels him. Physically. Emotionally. He is fed up with the endless arguments and fights. After all, he now knows, what makes his father tick. Always interfering in everything. Always knows everything better. And thinks nothing of him, the son. The latter unsettles the son. Finally, the son has to admit to himself, that his father has achieved something. Even if he likes to talk disparagingly about his father's position and income. He, the son, has not yet achieved anything. He is a little afraid whether he will ever make it like his father. He shudders at the thought of becoming like his father.

Before gymnasium starts and he can enjoy a breath of fresh air in Zurich and new freedoms, he will have to end his psychcological therapy with Miss Doctor L. at the Clinic Königsfelden, to hold through with his holiday job at the Cable Factory Brugg as an unskilled worker, where he is allowed to work, as he is over 14 years old, and to get through with the Confirmation Celebreation in the protestant church of Windisch.

One fine day the father had adressed the son and announced, that a serious talk were urgent. He were deeply worried about his, the son's, outbursts of rage and tantrums. Therefore he had registered him, the son, for a psychotherapy. The son gets immediately angry and shouts at the father, „Unbelievable! You are the one who is crazy and you force me to see a shrink!" The father keeps calm. He only adds, „The ‚shrink' is Miss Doctor L.!" The son shakes his head and walks off.

The son knows, that he makes a fool of himself, if he laments and complains about his father. The father, with his superficially friendly manner, is everyone's favourite and everyone falls for him, while he, the son, never really knows what people think of him. Sure, he gets on well with everyone and everyone seems to like him, but somehow he fears, that they don't take him serious. So he avoids to make a big fuss about his being forced to go to a psychotherapy. He only talks to his cousin Peider and his godfather, Uncle Peter, about it.

Godfather suggests, that the world won't end, if he, the son, complies to his fathers orders. After all he could complain in the therapy for hours about his father and the father had to pay for it. If he would refuse, new fights would arise. So it were clever just to do, what his father had suggested. This makes sense to the son.

Cousin Peider, the medical student, is surprised that the Little One's father, his Uncle Hans Günther, sends him, the Little One, in therapy to a psychcologist of the Königsfelden Clinic and a subordinate of his. The son shakes his head. That were no problem for him. He liked Miss Doctor L. very much and would gladly go to see her. Then Cousin Peider adds that it would certainly be exciting for him, the Little One, to finally find out what psychologists do to people who come to them for therapy. This argument also convinces the son.

The first therapy session is totally exciting for the son. Miss Doctor L. takes him through various tests. The Rorschach test, the Kraepelin. Now he finally knows what is behind these test names, that he often hears mentioned by the side from conversations at the family table. He agrees with Miss Doctor L. that he may contact her whenever he gets angry because of a fight with his father. This happens regularly. Then the son calls Miss Doctor L.. She usually asks him to come to her office immediately. The son hushes from his room through the patient wards, opening the for the patients closed doors with his passe-partout key. Scurries through various corridors and staircases of the clinic and through the men's wards A and C, where Miss Doctor L.'s office is at the end. Often he wears sunglasses, to hide his red eyes, after his rage had made him weep. In case he meets someone on the way. Miss Doctor L. listens patiently to the son, until he has calmed down. Then they talk about literature and theatre performances at the Kurtheater Baden. Afterwards, the son shuffles off in peace.

The sons main concern at the moment is his work in the Cable Factory Brugg during his springtime vacation, after the District School has ended and the gymnasium in Zurich not yet started. He is amazed, that his father shows interest in his doings. And enquieres, how he were doing at his manual job in the factory. He, the son, is allowed to talk about his experiences at the factory during a family dinner. Even the father listens attentively. Without ironic and mocking interjections.

"The work in the Cable Factory, ooo, ooo, ooo ! You can't imagine. Standing for hours at a machine, a kind of assembly line, where cables rushing through are wrapped with cords for insulation at a huge pace. My job is to make sure, that all the spools of cord are still sufficiently full. If a spool runs out of cord, I press a button to stop the machine. Replace the spool. Press the button again to start the machine again. And that's eight hours a day. Then the dust, the dirt. Yes, and then, just before the end of work Mr. S. put a broom in my hand today and said, before you leave, you'll mop the floor and sweep away the dirt. Mr. S. is my supervisor and quite nice. In his spare time he is, I'm not joking, president of the Rabbit Breeders' Association of Windisch and the surrounding area. I clean and clean in the sweat of my brow. Mr S. stops, watches me and doubles over laughing. ,The way you hold the broom in your hand! How can you hold a broom like that! I can't let you do it like that! You'll never get the floor clean. You hold a broom properly like that, and mop like that.' He demonstrates it to me and looks to see if I have now understood. Shakes his head again, corrects me. Corrects me once more. Remains quite friendly. Then he asks me, 'what are you doing in life? Are you such a semitariste?' Of course, he means seminarian. Probably because the only higher education he seems to know, is the teachers' seminary. What a gymnasium or an university is, is beyond his horizon. He doesn't even want it explained. Then he approaches me. He pats me consolatory on one of my shoulders. He looks me in the eye. With a friendly, encouraging look. 'Don't be sad. Even impractical people are useful somewhere. You too will make your way.' To imagine that a person's small world is enough and completely sufficient for him. That he doesn't have the slightest inferiority complex ..."

The father asks the son, if this is Mr S., who has a small house on the Reutenen street and is the father of two sons, one about his, the son's age. The son is irritated, that the father again seems to know people from the village, not socially, but professionally. That he, the son must once again assume, that Mr S. also is or was a patient of his father. Then the condescending attitude of his fahter towards these simple people from the village. How he hates the fate, that has given him this father, of all people, who stands out from the average and expects his son, to do the same.

As the Confirmation Celebration and the end of his vacation approaches, his holyday job at the Cable Factory comes to an end.

Before the confirmation would be celebrated, two crisis occurred, that ended in fights und the refusal of the son, to be confirmed.

Confirmation is preceded by two years of classes, given by the pastor, the Perparatory Class and the Confirmation Class. The son is not at all religious. He had attended Sunday School, because one attended it. He more or less enjoyed to listen to nice stories from the Bible, but couldn't and wouldn't believe in anything like God, Jesus or whatever. The first year with Preparatory Class was okay as well. A new experience. By and by he gets bored, specially in the last year, in the Confirmation Class.

The son dislikes the pastor. An acquaintance of the family. He finds him unctuous, unworldly, sanctimonious and mendacious. He is annoyed by the monotonous pious sayings and the Bible readings without discussions. The son blasphemes about the lessons at the lunch table. Imitates the pastor. Much to the delight of his sister Bettina. The father remarks mockingly, "The oh so clever Mister Son is too stupid to recognize and understand a true philosopher." The son knows that the father admires the pastor because he had studied philosophy as well as theology. And is considered one of the best taxpayers in the village, because of his marriage to a wealthy woman. The son swallows his anger at the father, who always agrees with the authority figures and never with him, the son.

Coincidally the son's class at the District School Brugg rehearses a pretty song, which one of the teacher has composed and which has the first line of the refrain 'Sleep, Gustav, sleep', for a school festival, When Confirmation Class in Windisch is once again utterly boring, the son, sitting in one of the front rows, turns around and murmurs, 'Pfuus, Guschti, pfuus' (Sleep, Gustav, sleep) to a fellow confirmand sitting in a back row, who is also his classmate in the District School in Brugg. The confirmation class acknowledges what they hear with laughter. As if stung by a tarantula, the pastor lunges at the son and smacks him. Of course, the father is amused by the fact that the pastor has put the son in his place and taught him decency. And the son declares, that he refuses to be confirmed. After the paster had requested a conversation with Doctor B., the father, the son is ordered by his father to apologize to the pastor for his unseemly behaviour. And the son has to promise his father, that he will continue to attend the Confirmation Class.

Crisis number two is brewing in Confirmation Class. A girl, fellow confirmand in his class no longer appears in the class. The girl has been shunned by everyone because she is short, ugly, stupid, unkempt, always smelly and, as is generally known, comes from a poor and bad background. The son feels sorry for the girl. He suspects that the girl has a lot of responsibility at home because, as is generally known in the village, her father drinks and her mother has sex with other men. The girl has to take care of her younger siblings. But somehow the son never gets close to the girl. When he approaches her, she rejects him harshly. The pastor reports with a sad and worried expression, that he had to exclude the girl from confirmation because she had strayed from the good path. Very soon word gets around, that the girl is pregnant and that this is why the paster refuses to confirmate her. When the son hears this, he explodes. He doesn't want to have anything to do with a church, that expells the poorest of the poor in a difficult situation. At the family dinner he declares, "I will quit Confirmation Class and refuse to be confirmated!"

The father grins at his son's outburst.

"I know the girl's family. If the priest made that decision, he will know why. About your confirmation: You're wrong, my young hero! In matters of religion you can only decide for yourself when you are sixteen, you are still fifteen, hahaha! I can force you to get your confirmation. Don't make such a fuss and don't disgrace us poor parents once more by talking bad about this most respectable pastor. Don't talk back, shut up!"

Confirmation day. In the morning the celebration at the Protestant Chur Windisch. At home then many gifts: A Hermes Baby typewriter, a Kodak Retina camera, several ties and three bottles of Old Spice aftershave. Then the traditional Confirmation Lunch with the confirmand, his godmother and his godfather with their families in a local restaurant. The son is quite angry, but shuts up. His father, instead of choosing for the Confirmation Lunch a local restaurant like all the others, choose, without asking his son ahead, if it were okay, a posh restaurant of a lodge brother from his Masonic Lodge. The father grins, "The restaurant is so nicely situated by the Hallwyl Lake. Does Windisch have a lake ? Njet, only the rivers Aare, Reuss and Limmat." When at this Confirmation Lunch in his honour also friends of his father appear, a couple the son does not like and the father knows the dislike of his son, the son was close to produce a tantrum, but suppressed it. At lunch in the posh restaurant, everyone is tidy and cheerful. A souvenir photo is snapped in the garden of the restaurant. The confirmand and his family. Father, mother, sister and confirmand. The father, proudly looking into the camera, hooks up with his two women, to his left his wife, to his right his daughter. On the left of the picture, although held by the mother, slightly off to the side is the son in a dark tailored suit with white shirt and tie in a posture as if he did not belong to the group, smiling for the photographer.

At home, after this Confirmation Lunch the father asks his son, "And does My Lord Son not bring a single word of thanks beyond his lips, after his old man spared no pains or expenses to celebrate The Lord Son worthily?"

The son can not hold back. He shouts, "What should I thank you for! That I had to be confirmed against my will! That my lunch had to take place not in Windisch in the Sonne Pub or the Harmony Restaurant, like everyone else's. But in such a distinguished establishment, run by your lodge brother! That you even invited against any tradition of such an occasion friends of yours!!!"

The father shouts immediately back, "Your exaggerations are disgusting! What have I done wrong that fate has given me such an ungrateful son, when I spoil him with the best of the best and want him to feel special?"

The son is intoxicated by what presents itself to him as an expedition into the big, wide world, which then becomes his everyday life. He had already been to Zurich several times before. At the Schauspielhaus Zurich, accompanied by his parents, to see 'Kabale und Liebe' and 'Wallenstein's Camp', plays written by Schiller. To buy those new-fangled blue jeans, not yet available in Windisch and Brugg, in a shop in Zurich, accompanied by his mother. To go pedalling on Lake Zurich in the company of a girl, a school friend, who is a grade above him in the District School Brugg and who is the envy of his schoolmates. But then he had felt completely lost in the big city. Now he can finally explore the city and experience new things. The new life begins with the fact that the gymnasium is no longer a ten-minute walk away from home.

On weekdays the son takes the train from Brugg to Zurich to go to the gymnasium in Zurich. More or less the same people are on the way every morning. Adults who work in Zurich. Students studying at the university.

Often Cousin Peider is also on the same train. The son gets to know countless people, even students, who are his seniors by several years. During the half-hour train ride, they smoke in company, chat, scribble down the last of their homework. Then there is also a beautiful girl from Brugg, whom the son so far only knew by sight. Her name is Eveline. Her father is a chief of bank in Brugg. She attends the School of Arts and Crafts in Zurich. Every now and then, the famous Professor von S. from the ETH Zürich (federal politechnical university), whom one knows from television and who lives in a castle nearby Brugg, also waits for the train on the platform. The sons godfather and Cousin Peider's father also takes the same train once a week, for his lectures as a professor at an institute in Zürich. When they travel together, they even exchanges a few words with the famous Professor von S., wo is an acquaintance of Godfather. Even the train journey to Zurich and back offers so many encounters with the most diverse people. The son is in his element.

Then the gymnasium in Zurich itself. In a venerable building on a small lane not far from the station and the famous Bahnhofstrasse. The son also finds the teachers so much more worldly and impressive than the teachers in small Brugg. At the District School Brugg, the sexes are segregated. At the gymnasium in Zurich, all classes are mixed. For the son, this was a tingly new feeling. As a new pupil from another canton with a different school system, the son ends up in a class that had already started four years ago. Everyone in his class knows each other very well. The class is a close-knit community. Most of the classmates come from Zurich or the surrounding area. The son joins his class as a newcomer and outsider. At the beginning, the son feels excluded. At the same time as the son, two other newcomers join the class. One, Urs, is also an outsider. The other, Marc, is from Zurich but doesn't know anyone in the class yet. The three newcomers get along well and become friends. They also gradually succeed in integrating into the class. Until then, the son had never had any difficulties finding his way around in different societies. When he overhears his classmates having private parties at weekends but not inviting them, the newcomers, the son complains to his cousin Peider, that he will never get used to this Zurich society. Cousin Peider urges the Little One not to hang his head at the slightest resistance. Now he has to approach people. He, Cousin Peider, had done it successfully at his time. By chance Cousin Peider knows one of the Little One's classmates, as she is the younger sister of one of his former classmates. Cousin Peider contactes his former classmate and tells her, that his little cousin feels snubbed by his Zurich classmates and is never invited to their private parties. From then on the son and his two new friends, who had joined the class at the same time, are included and fully integrated into the class. Even occupy special positions. Marc, because he is so clever. Urs, because he is so good-looking. The son, because he listens so well, especially to the girls in the class. The son hits the jackpot when he invites his whole class to Brugg for a visit to the cinema. In Zurich, the strict age limit for going to the cinema is eighteen. In Brugg, it is customary for teenagers to be let into the cinema after they have left the District School, at fifteen or sixteen. The son's calssmates are enthusiastic. Even the boys put up with the fact that the film they get to see in the Cinema Excelsior in Brugg is 'Sissi' with Romy Schneider as the empress Elisabeth from Austria. Not really a boy's film. When James Bond Dr. No comes to the cinema they are old enough to go to the cinema in Zurich. The mother enthusiastically feeds the pack from Zurich after they have seen ‚Sissi'. The father willingly opens his wine cellar and gets to know his son's classmates.

The son knows that he must not say a word to his father about his initial difficulties integrating into the new class. He would ridicule him and tell him, it were his own fault. He, the father, never had forced him to go to the sinfully expensive private gymnasium in Zurich. Fights between father and son decrease drastically. Occasionally a minor fight flares up, mostly revolving around money. The son is annoyed with his stingy father. The father counters the son's exaggerated demands with remarks like, "just you wait, they'll straighten out your mutton legs" or "when you stand on your own two feet, you'll learn how sourly money is earned". The son carefully tells his father that one of his classmates is a ‚Baroness Von and Zu' from Munich. Because her parents are usually away all over the world, she lives with her siblings in a villa with a butler. She could order this butler to write excuses for school as she wished. Because she misses so much school, her performance is not so good. When exams are due, she often sits down next to him, the son, and writes them off. The father insists on knowing the baroness's full name. Then he pulls out a book from his library, the Gotha Nobility Directory, and enlightens the son about the history of this noble family. On this occasion, the father is so mild-mannered that the son can easily interject, that he saw a fine, but, alas, very expensive, Parker fountain-pen in the window of the Landolt and Arbenz Stationery Shop on Bahnhofstrasse. His friend Urs had been given such a pen by his parents. So, the son comes across this beautiful Parker fountain-pen and is blissfully happy. Even his father has to admit that his son's handwriting has improved with this fountain-pen and is exquisite now. The son's mother comments, "Rainer's handwriting is so nice and legible, unlike yours, Hansel, which, despite your Pelikan fountain-pen, only I, as an insider, can decipher, but only with the greatest difficulty!"

On Mondays Godfather gives lectures in Zurich. His tradition is to have lunch on these Mondays at the Seilbähnli (Cable Car) Restaurant, where rustic Swiss food is served. The old waitress always looks carfefully after the professor and his company with pleasure. If the son feels like it and has time, he is always a welcome guest of Godfather on these Mondays. The son enjoys these meals and especially the conversations with Godfather. Sometimes Cousin Peider and other cousins, who are studying in Zurich, also join in.

The father suggests, that the son attend during his summer holidays a holiday course in French at the University of Lausanne, in order to improve his French. He could then stay with a cousin of Mummy and his family in Vevey. The son hates, when his father is trying to organize him. Nevertheless, he studies the prospectus of the holiday course. He learns, that it consists mainly of lectures on contemporary French literature. He is immediately hooked. In order not to loose his face, he pretends to reluctantly sacrifice his summer holidays for this holiday course in French, as he already were very good in French. He only agreed, to please his father. His father is pleased. The son, in reality, is almost bursting with joy and excitement. He also finds it totally cool to go in and out of a real university as a pupil of a gymnasium and to attend to lectures like a real university student.

When the son had been younger, his father provided him with books to read, that he, the father, thought were appropriate for his son. The father's huge library is taboo for the son and also his sister. "How dare you touch my books with your dirty hands", "Did you make those dog-ears in the book pages?" and "Unbelievable that a sensible boy can't refrain from scribbling in books!". But secretly, the son and his friends raid his father's library in his absence. They know very well that on the middle bookcase on the top shelf on the right, which they can only reach with the help of a chair, are the medical books and the sex education books, in which there are pictures of naked bodies, including the lower bodies of men and women. While the father's readings remain a secret for the son, because the father does not talk about them, he learns about contemporary Swiss authors from Godfather, Aunt Bertie and Cousin Peider. Cousin Peider also introduces him to the novel 'Ilona' by Hans Habe and 'Le petit Prince' by Saint-Exupéry. Mummy reads mainly detective novels, Agatha Christie and Edgar Wallace, has all their paperbacks, which the father notes with a certain amount of sarcasm. The son very much enjoys his regular visits to the theatre, the Kurtheater in Baden, accompanied by his father and/or Mummy, Godfather, Aunt Bertie. The son is fascinated by a performance of Gerhart Hauptmann's 'Michael Kramer' as a guest performance from Vienna. He can hardly believe how the son suffers humiliation at the hands of his father in the play. The content of the play is not discussed with the father after the performance. The father elatedly recounts, how he had corresponded with Gerhart Hauptmann about his own poetry in the early 1930s. With Yvette, the French au pair of Aunt Bertie and Godfather, the son learns enough French to understand texts. The French language fascinates him. At the gymnasium in Zurich, French lessons are supplemented by literature. The son finds the French teacher, Monsieur J., brilliant. The son comes across Albert Camus' L'étranger and is fascinated. With his new friend Urs he explores French literature from Camus, Mauriac and Malraux to Gide and Sartre. He also attends all the theatre premieres at the Schauspielhaus Zurich with his friend Urs. In the back row, in the stalls or, with a bit of luck, on a folding seat on the side of one of the front rows. At a German-language premiere of a play by Peter Ustinov, they recognize the author in the audience and even manage to get his autograph. When it comes to literature and theatre visits, the son is able to escape his father's dictates and finally follow his own inclinations.

In the holiday course at the Lausanne University the topic is 'Le nouveau roman' (new novels). One lecture is even about Albert Camus' La peste. The son attends every single lecture, buys all the books covered by the lecutres. He revels in material that is not taught to him at the gymnasium in Zurich. He learns about 'Le Planétarium' by Natalie Sarraute, 'La Modification' by Michel Butor and 'Dans le labyrinthe' by Alain Robbe-Grillet. Later, as a film screening of the Zurich Middle School Film Club – every Wednesday during school break at midday in the cinema Corso – he will see the film 'L'année dernière à Marienbad', for which Alain Robbe-Grillet wrote the screenplay. This film, of which his parents take no notice, is a cult film for the son and his friends. Not least because of the game with matches that appears in it. The son revels in his newfound world, which he shares with his friends. As long as he has enough money to buy French pocket books ‚livres de poche' and records with songs by Edith Piaf, Juliette Gréco, Jeanne Moreau, Colette Renard and Lotte Lenya, buy tickets for the theatre and the films, there are no more arguments with his father. The father merely admonishes the son not to neglect over his obsession with French and literature his studies for school and especially for the scientific subjects, in which he is weak.

The son appreciates, that his father and Mummy are sociable people, run an open house and love company above all else. The son and also his sister are allowed to bring friends home at will. The parents are happy to meet their children's friends. The father turns up his nose when the son brings friends who seem improper to him. The son loves, when guests are invited to dinner at home. Then it usually gets exciting. Often there are interesting people at the table. This time, the wife of a young doctor colleague of the father from the Königsfelden Clinic is invited for dinner. She works as a secretary in the clinic. Her husband is currently in military service. To the son's immense delight, this woman, who is sitting at the family table, comes from the French-speaking part of Switzerland. She has a degree in French from the University of Lausanne. In no time, the young woman and the son are involved in an animated discussion in French about the 'nouveau roman' (new novels – a specific term to indicate modern, living French authors, the ones that the son had got to know during his holiday course at the Lausanne University) in general, without mentioning names of specific authors. Mummy and the son's sister listen. The father, who understands some French but has no real command of the language, interjects from time to time in German with ironic remarks or remarks questioning the thoughts of the young woman and his son. So the conversation alternates between French and German. The son, much to the father's astonishment and delight, spontaneously responds to one of the father's critical remarks. This leads to a lively discussion about the characteristics of the 'nouveau roman'. The son shakes his head at some of his father's remarks. The father sticks to his statements. The young woman defends the son's views. The father joyfully argues with his son and does not spare ironic turns of phrase and clever sayings of a true humanist. The son, instead of countering an assertion of his father, looks at him calmly and asks, what he, the father, actually understands by 'nouveau roman', a term clearly defined in the French cultural sphere.

" Thomas Mann, of course! Who else! "

The young woman and the son cast meaningful glances at each other. The son would like to burst out laughing. The young woman is obviously embarrassed by the situation. Mummy saves the situation by offering the bowl of peas and carrots and asking the guest to take another bite.

The parents often travel during father's vacations. They go on long-distance trips on their own. Without their children. Who are then entrusted to the care of Godfather and Aunt Bertie, who live in the same house, one floor below. Family holidays are spent in hotels in Switzerland or in the south of France or Italy by the sea. Years ago, the son was allowed to travel alone to Stuttgart, where he was met at the station by his godmother, Aunt Ilse, his father's sister. She lives in Bad Cannstatt. When in the gymnasium in Zurich, the son is independent enough and plans his own travels. Together with his friend Urs. As they both are crazy about the French culture, French literature, French films, their first destination has to be Paris. Both parents believe, their sons are to young to travel on their own abroad. The son and Urs arrange a meeting of their partens in the Select Restaurant in Zurich. There they convince them, that they are fluent in the French language and that at 16 they are old enough to take care of themselves. The resistence of both parents is quickly broken. The son and his friend Urs are allowed to travel to Paris. There they see and hear Edith Piaf on her last 'Tour de Chant' at the Olympia. When the son, after the trip, reminisces Edith Piaf and makes his parents hear the record he has bought, the father finds it strange, that anyone could take a liking to such a croaky voice. Godfather says that he had already heard Piaf once during his stay in Paris in the 1930s and had been deeply impressed by her charisma.

Many of father's relatives live spread all over the world. The son gets to know some of these relatives, when they visit Switzerland and the family. He knows well Aunt Senta, a cousin of the father, and her husband, Uncle Fritz, from London. Uncle Fritz had owned a publishing house in Leipzig. Then the family had moved to England in the late 30s. The son likes this aunt and uncle very much. They invite him to visit them London. If he liked, together with his friend Urs. The father pays for the trip and grants a to the utmost surprise of the son generous pocket money. Groaning, "My son's demands will make me, his poor father, a beggar!"

When the son and his friend Urs are in London, they learn, that Aunt Senta's and Uncle Fritz' youngest daughter, Gaby, whom the son knows, since she had spent holidays in Switzerland, has got married in Canada. The son sits in the kitchen and watches Aunt Senta preparing dinner. He asks her, how Gaby's wedding in Canada had been. Aunt Senta says, "The wedding must have been very nice, I hear".
"Then you weren't there?"

"Nah."

"Sure. All that travelling just for a wedding."

"Boy, what times are you living in. The journey from London to Vancouver is a stone's throw by plane. We didn't want to be there because Gaby got married Catholic for her husband's sake."

"All right. For us Protestants, especially old people like you, a marriage between Protestants and Catholics is still inacceptables.Not so for me. I had a Catholic girlfriend, and we used to go cuddling in a confessional at the Catholic church in Brugg ..."

"We are Jewish. Not Protestants. Don't you know, that your German grandparents were born Jews? Okay, you just hadn't known them anymore. Don't look at me with such astonishment. So, this is new to you? Then you probably don't know how your German Omi (grandmother) had died in Germany. No, no, it's not up to me to tell you. Ask your father, when you get home. Let him tell you!"

The son does not want to push Aunt Senta to tell him more about his German Omi and Opa. So far, he had only perceived them as distant protagonists in his father's stories of the past. But never as real people connected to him, the son. The son realizes how he had always found his father's rapturous tales of earlier times in Silesia boring, embarrassing and alien. The first car that Opa had bought in 1910 and initially chauffeured himself until he steered it into the ditch. From then on, the former coachman was trained as a chauffeur. Stories repeated and heard a thousand times. How he had had a much better living back home in his beloved Silesia. Why, for heaven's sake didn't he then stay there! Then came the tales of the countless journeys of Omi and Opa. Whereby the father, when he was old enough, accompanied the parents as their chauffeur. The father's sporting achievements as a youth and young man in fencing, riding and shooting. As far as the son can remember, he never saw his father actively practising a sport. Not even riding a bicycle. Missing from these stories of the father - and not only the father, but also all the other German close relatives - are the war years. The death of Omi and Opa. The leaving of Silesia. The son had never asked any questions about it. Nor about the fact, that and why several relatives on his father's side live in England, in the USA, in Argentina, in Australia, in Israel. The son has accumulated knowledge about his Swiss relatives, as it were, along the way, in everyday life and in his dealings with people. He experiences this environment as his extended family. While the German relatives stand like foreign entities in the son's big enough world. The son asks himself, whether he can dare to talk to his father about the death of his Omi and Opa in Germany. Or whether again he will make a terrible mistake and be harshly rebuked.

The son's attempt to learn more about his father's difficulties during the Nazi time and the war fails. "No time." "That's not an issue now." "How dare you ask such a question in public, where anyone can hear!" Mummy, who overhears the the son questioning his fahter, coolly throws at the son as he comes to her in the kitchen like a beaten dog, "Now don't make that face! Even you should understand, that no one likes to talk about the fact that his mother, your Omi, was murdered in Auschwitz."

The son is confused by the new knowledge, with which he can do little and which he cannot and will not share with anyone. He is ashamed, that he knows too little and almost nothing. Despite the now even to him obvious facts. He knows that if he asks his Swiss relatives, they refer him to his father. And his father does not want to talk about it. Not even with his Godmother, the sister of his father, with whom he can otherwise talk about so many things, can he talk about these things. To appropriate questions she replies, "Oh forget it, I can't talk about it, or I'll start crying."

The son knows that his father likes to browse around bookshops in Aarau or Baden in his spare time. The father knows all the good bookshops in the region and also the booksellers personally. The bookshop visits usually take a long time. The other family members, if they don't have other things to do in Aarau or Baden while the father is rummaging around in the bookshop, detest accompanying the father on his trips to Aarau or Baden. The father, on the other hand, hates nothing so much as going on an excursion on his own. He needs company. One Saturday afternoon, the father insists on going to the bookshop in Aarau. Mummy is busy elsewhere. Sister Bettina is at a friend's. Mummy implores the son to please his father for once. Who only means well for him. And to accompany him to Mr. F.'s bookshop in Aarau. The son only grumbles briefly to his Mummy. When his father asks at lunch on a Saturday if anyone would like to accompany him to Aarau in the afternoon, the son meekly declares that he is willing. His father is delighted.

The son has not the least aversions against bookshops. Not even a long stay in a bookshop bothers him. On the other hand, he never really feels comfortable when he is alone in company with his father. It starts with the father always sitting so tense behind the wheel of his Austin Cambridge. If there are other people with him, the son pays no attention to it. But when they are on their own, the son is fixated on the father's cramping. Fortunately, the father does not make the suggestion that the son, who is taking driving lessons, get behind the stearing wheel. If his father were sitting next to him, he would make out of nervous tension every possible mistake while driving. So, the son sits dutifully in the passenger seat on the drive to Aarau and wonders whether his father will invite him to the Brändli Tea Room for an ice cream after the visit to the bookshop. With this question he immediately remembers something a classmate of his had recently said. This classmate had confessed to him, that he was most embarrassed, when his father invited him, only him, to the noble Kronenhalle Restaurant for lunch and they sat at a table, the two of them, father and son. He imagined that other people might assume, that an old gay man is out with his young lover. This stupid saying now stiucks in the son's head and also inhibits him, when he is out alone with his father in public.

The father talks to Mr F., the owner of the bookshop in Aarau, whom he knows well and holds in high esteem. Mr F. draws the father's attention to several new and interesting publications. The conversation clearly revolves around books that interest the two old men. By exchanging glances with the bookseller, smiling and nodding, the son skilfully manages to distance himself from the two of them in decorum and to find the books that interest him in the well-stocked bookshop with many side rooms and countless racks. He gets stuck in the French books section. After some time, he notices a cupboard with a closed glass door. This cupboard obviously contains the most valuable and beautiful books. At first glance, the son recognizes that they are editions from the Bibliothèque de la Pléiade. Elsewhere, he had held once in his hands one of these magnificent thin-print volumes bound in leather with discreet beige edges. The son stands on his toes. There is a complete edition of Albert Camus' writings in one volume. Camus, along with Brecht, is his idol. He knows Caligula's monologue to the moon by heart. The first sentence of 'L'étranger', 'Aujourd'hui, maman est morte' almost puts him into a trance. 'Il faut imaginer Sisyphe heureux', the last sentence from 'Le Mythe de Sisyphe', speaks from his heart. In the French lesson they had discussed fundamentally 'le problème zu choix' with the French teacher, Monsieur J., based on Camus' philosophy. The son is jolted out of his reverie by his father's voice.

"My offspring would like to have a closer look at that book," the son hears his father say to Mr F..

"Certainly, Doctor B., certainly ..."

Mr F. moves the key. Fetches the book from the cupboard. Hands the book to the son. The son can hardly believe it. He holds this precious book in his hands. In his hands! Hardly dares to touch it properly, to open it, for fear of soiling the book.

"Do you want this book?" his father asks.

"No, no, no," the son stammers. "Much, much too precious for me and expensive ..."

To his utmost surprise and joy the son gets the book as a gift from his father. He no longer needs to let it out of his hands. The son would have liked to spontaneously fall around his father's neck. He is so moved. He would have liked to hug him tightly, very tightly. The father's posture and facial expression command the son not to make a fuss. Just to say thank you quietly, in a trembling voice. The son understands. Anything else would have been effeminate. And a disgrace, not just in public.

The son is annoyed that everyone pesters him, what he is going to study after the gymnasium. His obvious choice would be to study philology, French language and literature. But for all his love of books of French authors, the idea of having to listen as a university student to gossip of renowned professors about books and authors and later as a teacher having to let out such gossip himself nauseates him. Monsieur J., the French teacher, had once thrown out, out of enthusiasm for one of the son's essays, that he, the son, were a born writer. Now he dreams of being a writer. He writes short stories and theatre plays. That he only shows to his friends. But never to his parents.

The son's parents couldn't hardly miss to notice their son's enthusiasm for the theatre. They were alarmed. They feared th worst. In order to prevent their son from getting the idea of becoming an actor, the father asked a friend, who is an artist, to warn his son, how important in life it were, to have a decent profession first, to study at university, and only then devout oneself to art. For Mummy and Aunt Bertie it was absolutely clear, that the Little One had to study law and then join the diplomatic service. Aunt Bertie had a good acquaintance, who is an ambassador, and therefore she sees the the Little One as an ambassador as well. Given his, the Little One's, talent on the social stage and his good looks. The father, on the other hand, urges the son to study medicine. Out of tradition. He, the father, and the son's grandfather, the father's Vatel, had been doctors. And never had regretted it. The vehemently uttered request of the father, that almost resembled an order, catapulted the son in a tantrum. „I never ever will study medecine!" The son's tantrum provoked a tantrum of the father. Much shouting was heard in the whole house As this encounter happened to take place in the son's room, this time the father leaves the room, slamming the door. When the son sneaks into the kitchen, where Mummy is preparing the dinner, she sighs, "I had so hoped that the time of your awful fights was definitely over. Please, please, don't fight again with your father! I always get in between the two of you. I don't understand, why you always have to fight. You are so much alike." Mummy's remark infuriates the son anew. But he controls himself. He leaves the kitchen without a word. And without slamming the door.

The grandfather of Marc, the son's friend, had been a judge at the Federal Court and had written clever books. Marc decides to study law. So does the son.

Among the son's friends, who are mainly recruited from former classmates of the gymnasium in Zürich or a few of the District School Brugg, critisism for the military is widespread, but a definite refusal to do the compulsary military service is not a real issue. At most, there are exchanges about how one could be exempted from military service for medical reasons and how stupid one would have to be at recruit school to avoid getting the proposal to continue military service and become an officer. Cousin Peider, the jock, is not accepted in military service because of a medical diagnosis, Scheuermann, a bad back. Godfather reminds the son, that it is an advantage professionally and socially to be an officer in the army. On the other hand, once a recruit in the army, the, the son, has to decide for himself, whether he wants to become an officer or not. Recruit school has never done any harm to a young man. The father, who admires anything military and uniforms, works on the son, how important it is to strive for the officer's rank. He also asks friends, brothers from his Masonic lodge, to take the son into prayer and make him understand, that there is no alternative to the officer's grade. The father's posturing annoys the son.

"You're not a real Swiss, just a bought-in Swiss," the son accuses the father. "You don't know how things work here and now with the military! So shut up!"

"The son who knows everything better and yet doesn't have a clue about toots and bows!" the father counters in a louder voice, which sets off an argument that makes Mummy sigh once more.

At weekends, the son comes home from recruit school. The proud father picks his son in uniform up in his car from the barracks. Usually, the son's comrades, who are heading for the railway station, come along for a part of the journey. The father wants to know everything, especially from the son's comrades, about everyday life in the barracks. About drill and about service with the weapon. The son's comrades, most of whom come from simpler backgrounds, enjoy being questioned and taken in their stride by this so open and friendly Doctor B.. They repeatedly emphasize to the son, how they envy him for his nice father. One of them, in the back of the Austin Cambridge, sings the song that they had shouted at the top of their lungs on a night march, 'Das Leben ist ein Würfelspiel" (Life is a game of dice). The son, who is sitting in the rear of the car, notices in the rear-view mirror how his father's expression is distorted. His father is obviously totally displeased with something. The son has no clue, what it is. But is not really astonished, that his father keeps quiet in the company of others and doesn't start to scold him, the son.

At lunch, the mood at the table is relaxed. The father even points out, how proud he is to see his son in uniform.

"What I forgot to ask your comrades and I had wanted to ask, how is the food in the barracks," the father jovially turns to the son with a mischievous grin.

"Oh, okay for me. The others grumble terribly. The fourier miscalculated, now his budget is exhausted. He can hardly buy fresh food anymore. Has to use up the cheap canned goods, the army is compelled to have in stock. Now almost every day we have 'gestampfter Jud' (crushied Jew – a in military traditional, common and popular local expression in vernacular for tinned minced meat, which nobody, who uses the expression, associates with Jews), sometimes with tomato sauce, sometimes mashed or fried, with pasta or potatoes. I like it. Most of my comrades think it's terrible."

The son babbles happily. The cheerfulness suddenly fades from his father's face. The father stares at the tablecloth. Wipes his mouth clean with his napkin. Stands up. Wordlessly leaves the dining room and disappears into his study. Mummy covers her face with both hands. Sighs in a whisper with a tearful voice, " Boy, boy, how could you say ‚gestampfter Jud' in front of your father. You should have shown more respect for his history. You should have known, that your father, your Omi... Your father had already told me how shocked he had been, when you and your comrades sang 'Das Leben ist ein Würfelspiel' at the top of your lungs. That terrible song from Germany and the Nazi era!"

The son is outraged that he unvoluntarily offends his father, when he just behaves and speaks as any normal Swiss man behaves and speaks, who has been in the army. Not even Mummy, who is Swiss – born Swiss, Swiss of origin and having been in the army – understands him. She always takes sides with his father.

The son survives recruit school. He gets to know comrades from all walks of life in close quarters. He and a few other fellow recruits, who happen to be university student, manage to behave so stupidly in the recruit exams, that no proposal to continue the military service with the officers school is given to them. The son is happy. He will be a simple soldier all his life long. To celebrate this, the son and his buddies get drunk with much beer in the popular and not at all elegant Zum scharten Eck (at the sharp corner) Pub. The father is outraged when he hears, that his son failed to get the proposal to become an officer. The son can live with his father's indignation and devotes himself to his studies at university again. That is, he devotes himself above all to ingenious networking with fellow male, but as well female students and also students from other faculties in the Rondell, the coffee bar in the university's main building.

Shortly before the end of the spring semester at university and the start of the son's summer holidays, the father blithely informs the son at a family dinner, that he, the son, should report to Doctor K., the president of the District Court in Brugg. Tomorrow at 3 o'clock p.m.. That a surprise awaited him there. A traineeship for two months at a real law court.

"Now, don't make such a face," the father continues. "It must be a pleasure for a budding lawyer to be able to apply his acquired knowledge at university in the real world. Yesterday I approached Doctor K. in the Sternen Club about this possibility. He said, it would be an honour for him, if you did a traineeship with him. And it is to your best, when you don't waste your time on useless things. It doesn't seem to have occurred to you, that it can only be an advantage to gain all kinds of professional experience early on. After all, you want to make a career, don't you? Why else would we have let you study!"

For the sake of peace and quiet, the son doesn't rebel. He just mentions laconically, that he can bury his nice holiday plans. To his relief, no one asks, what his holiday plans are. So far he has none.

The traineeship at the District Law Court Brugg turns out to be not bad at all. At the same time as the son, another university student is working there as a trainee. The son knows this other trainee by sight. As he also travels back and forth by train from Brugg to Zurich. The son knows, that the other one is two years his senior and studies a few semesters above him. He has already passed his first exams at university. Until now he has never talked to him. The younger students use to admire the older ones in awe and usually do not dare to adress them. The son and the other trainee get along very well here at the court. They have much to talk about.

The introduction to the traineeship at the court is brief. The law court clerk assigns the work to the trainees. The son has an insight into files. Has to prepare reports for the judges. Some files contain interesting stories, unimaginable and mindblowing details about people and their actions. Dr. K., judge and president of the court and friend of the son's father, greets the two trainees on the very first day in the morning. Later, in the afternoon, Dr K. calls the son to his office.

Dr. K. confesses to the son, that he is in a dilemma. He explains, that the Department of Justice in Aarau had only approved one trainee position. Theoretically, it would be possible, since the position is now double-occupied, to halve the salary so that each trainee gets half the salary. However, the other trainee comes, as the son certainly knows, from a very humble background. He must earn some money. Grinning, Dr. K. adds with a wink that he, the son, comes from a good stable and could easily do without the salary, for a good cause. So that the other, needy trainee could enjoy the entire wage. The son would have felt shabby not to agree with this proposition. Gritting his teeth, he forces himself to grin and casually and cheerfully throws down, "Sure, I am glad to renounce to my share!"

In the evening at home, the son goes on a rant about his father. He accuses him of being the cause of never ending disadvantages because of his, the father's, position and autocratic behaviour. Without him he could have a holiday job that pays well and make a nice trip afterwards.

"Please don't shout like that! To make such a fuss about money ! It's ridiculous to be attached to merely money!"

"Your arrogance makes me puke!"

"If the aristocratic son of proletarian parents doesn't consider the simple Sicily group tour with the Akademische Reisen (academic travels) below his dignity, we might invite him to accompany us on this journey after the end of his traineeship," the father says in his familiar tone.

196

A trip with a group of old people is not at all, what the son has dreamt of. Sicily would be okay. And this trip will certainly cost the father a lot of money. Besides, it would give him the chance to stay in famous and expensive hotels. The son agrees to the deal, growling in mock disgust.

After the son's traineeship some days are left, until the trip to Sicily starts. The son is during a fine day by chance alone at home. The telephone rings. The Manager of Akademische Reisen asks to speak to Doctor B. The son says, his father were at work, not at home. The man on the phone asks, if he had by chance the honour to speak to the son, of Doctor B., Mr Rainer B.. He were amused by the coincidence. Because finally he had to discuss something with him, the son of Doctor B. He now explains to the son, that every group tour were accompanied by two guides, a scientific guide and an administrative guide. The scientific guide were a renowned professor of Italian history. But, alas, the administrative guide had fallen ill. He had to be replaced. He, the Manager of Akademische Reisen, were in a big distress, to find in no time an appropriate administrative guide. The administrative tour guide only had a few tasks. Such as allocating rooms in the hotels. Confirming reservations for meals in restaurants, reconfirming flights and so on. As a university student, he, the son, should be quite capable of carrying out this activity easily. Without having to give up the sightseeing part of the tour. Of course, if the son would accept to be the administrative guide on the tour, his share of the travel expenses would be reimbursed. The son says yes to the deal. He tells the man the name of his bank and the number of his account there.

The son recounts at the family dinner, that he will be the administrative tour guide on the Sicily trip. The Manager of the Akademische Reisen had made clear, that the reimbursed amount of money were his salary for this function and therefore were transmitted to his account. Mummy laughs heartily and exclaims, "You've been lucky again – what a lucky man!". Whereupon the father, who had previously listened to the son's explanations with a serious expression and had thought up appropriate words of protest about the way the money is flowing, now, for Mummy's sake, renounces to protest. As his Little Monster thinks, it's okay like that. The son notes with amusement that the father is about to resign himself to the fact that he, the son, can usually charm people, get the best for himself and live happily. A quarrel and shadow fight between father and son is bypassed this time.

10.

The father has to accept, willy-nilly, that his son can usually charm people, get the best for himself and sit back comfortably. The son clearly lacks grit and ambition. He takes the path of least resistance. Does not take control of his destiny. His pointless refusals to study medicine, to become an officer in the military, as befits any decent Swiss and academic, are annoying for his father. Instead, the son pursues diffuse dreams of being an artist, builds castles in the air, that are like soap bubbles. At least the son has finished his law studies. But what would have happened after his graduation if he, the father, had not intervened, is written in the stars! The father arranges for his son to get a job as adjunct in the practice of a friend of his, the renowned Barrister H., a former judge at the Cantonal Court in Aarau. The father prepares himself for the son's worst reaction. But the son's reaction proves to be mild. He takes up the job. He leaves home and moves to his own flat in the village Windisch. On most Sundays, he comes home for lunch.

"And, how is the work at Barrister H.'s practice", the father asks.

"It's an experience. I see, that the job of an attorney is not my thing at all. Barrister H. is a shrewd crook and has a drinking problem."

"Now you've only been working there a few weeks and already this defeatism!"

"Why don't you never ask me, what my thing is? I want to write. I am a writer. Monsieur J., my former French teacher, had attested me a talent for writing. Why are you, who make such a fuss about high literature, so against me being a writer?! Yes, yes, to you culture is but a trendy and fashionable entertainment. No member of your family should dare to be an artist! Barrister H. is a perfect character for a novel."

"Interesting, interesting. My son, a writer! Look at that. Where are your publications? Are you already making money with it? Are you already famous without me having heard about it?! Exactly. Once you are famous, I too will be proud, that my son is a writer!"

The father cannot help but scold his son in front of his mother.

"He's a bloody show-off!"

"He gets that from you," the mother promptly retorts, only to follow up with, "Sorry, Hansel. If someone wants to hold his own in his world and stand out, he has to have something to offer. And talk about what he has to offer. Big mouth, perhaps. But often there is more to it than meets the ears. Don't be too harsh and quick in demonizing the show-offs!"

From the mother, to whom the son tells a little more about his life than to him, the father, the father learns, that the son has meanwhile given up his job with Barrister H. and has a new position at a Zurich court. There he earns four times as much and can finally pay for his flat. The father does not interfere any more. Not even when the son announces after a little over a year, that he will be travelling during some months through India with his friend Marc. The father no longer understands these young people. He takes it in his stride that the mother, Peter, Bertie, Peider and all are on the son's side. At least, the son pays for his living and his crazy trip to India out of his own earnings. The father doesn't know whether the mother and others are still giving him some money. Even the father then is touched by how the son regularly writes letters about his experiences on his trip to India and with buses back trough Afghanistan, Iran and Turkey, which lasted several months, and asks his parents to keep these letters for him at all costs. Because they are, as it were, his travel diary. The father has to admit that his son can write. After the trip to India is over luckily, the son does not even grumble, when the father points out to him that it is customary in his, the father's, family for the men to do their doctorate. The son succeeds, which reassures the father, in finding a topic for his dissertation with a quite prominent doctoral supervisor, Professor N., who is known for his originality.

"How did you ever get this famous Professor N. to take you as a doctoral student," the father asks the son.

"This friend, Max, is a friend of Professor N.'s. Professor N. visits Max all the time, drinks away his Chivas Regal. Max then proposed to me, that I come and visit too, the next time Peter N. comes to visit him. That's how I got to know Professor N. personally. Max has asked him to suggest a possible topic for my dissertation and to be my doctoral supervisor. Professor N. said, this procedure was not usual at all. Doctoral students had to find their topics on their own. But he just had a topic in store, that he would like to see examined in a dissertation. That's how I came to my topic, actually by chance ..."

The father shakes his head and can hardly believe how his son seems to meander effortlessly through his life. Even the twist with the part-time job. One fine day the son turned up and declared, he had a part-time job in the Cantonal Administration in Zurich.

"Don't talk nonsense," the father throws out, annoyed. "I've never heard of such a thing as part-time jobs, at least not for men."

"There really haven't been so far," the son explains with a grin. "At random, I had called the Human Resources of the Department of Finance of the Canton Zurich. I had heard that the public sector was having difficulties recruiting lawyers. I was told straight away to hold the line and I was put through to the Chief of the Department of Finances. He asked me, what kind of job I was looking for. He said he had a vacancy for a lawyer. A little more than an hour ago, a young lawyer had contacted him, who showed interest in this position, but only wanted to work part-time, because he was writing a dissertation on the side. I explained, that I was in the same situation. Then the Chief said, if I were interested to share my job with this other lawyer, he would try to fight with the Human Resources for the splitting of the job in two parttime jobs. This never had been done so far in the Public Administration of the Canton Zürich, but he will, out of need, fight for it. And he were sure, to be successful with his request."

The father is amazed at what has fallen again into his son's lap. A few years later - good things come to those who wait - the son reports that he has now submitted his dissertation to Professor N. and that he has accepted it. He recommended it to the faculty for approval.

"Now the thing is," the son begins hesitantly. "I have a job, I do earn some money, but after the approval of the dissertation by the faculty of the university, you have to turn in 250 printed copies for all the libraries. And these printing costs ..."

"I always had promised," the father interrupts the son, "that I will pay for the printing of your dissertation ..."

"That's sweet, really sweet," the son now interrupts his father, "but I have a suggestion. It is normal to deliver the manuscript in its raw form to the publishing house that is specialized in printing dissertations. That costs so-and-so much. But now there is also the possibility of producing the print-ready manuscript yourself according to the publisher's exact specifications, if you have a good typewriter at your disposal. New on the market is the IBM ballpoint typewriter, which is perfect for producing a beautiful print-ready fair copy manuscript and submitting it to the publisher. Then the printing in the publishing house costs only a fraction. Even with the purchase of an IBM ball-head typewriter with proofreading ribbon, the latest of the new on the market, the printing costs of the dissertation are much lower than if you submit the raw manuscript to the publisher, and they make the artwork themselves."

"That is to say, the young son is blackmailing his old father," the father presses out with a serious expression, but put on in jest. "Write down the figures for me, please. If they convince me, you'll get your IBM ball-head typewriter. Ball-head, you say? That's not the latest thing, son! Around 1900, Vatel, my father, your grandfather, had given his father, your great-grandfather, the typewriter that was all the rage at the time, a Blickensderfer typewriter. It had a ballpoint head, but only one key and a lever by means of which you set the type wheel to the desired letter and then pressed the key ..."

The son is now a doctor of law and has his IBM ballpoint typewriter. The father is proud. The son quits his job. Which, of course, worries the father.

"Quit, yes and no. My colleague with whom I shared the job till now has found a new job. Now the Chief of the Department of Finances, my superior, said that I now had my doctorate and was no longer dependent on the part-time position. Either I was ready to work full time or lose the job. If I chose the second option, he said, he was prepared to give me notice so that I could immediately draw unemployment benefits until I found a new job."

"No way! Work-shy, my son! Won't work full time like all normal people do! You can't expect a penny from me! See for yourself how you get on!"

A little later, the father reads in the programme preview of Swiss radio that 'Portrait of an impossible relationship. Minute Dramolet by Rainer B.', is being broadcast. The short radio play, reads the father, is a commissioned work by Swiss Radio in collaboration with several local businesses, which set up listening stations in their shops, where the short radio plays by thirty authors can be listened to. On the radio, all thirty radio plays will be broadcast one after the other. Afterwards, the radio plays will also be printed in the daily newspaper on thirty days. One radio play per day. With a portrait of the author. The father is amazed and can hardly believe that his good-for-nothing son has made it onto the radio.

"Crap, crap, crap!"
"What is it, Hansel?"

"Oh, my Little Monster, now a short radio play by Rainer is going to be broadcast on the radio. And I happen to be then at a meeting in the Masonic Lodge in Aarau. The exact time is given for the broadcast, at 8.37 p.m.! There's nothing I can do about this stupid meeting! There's no way I can chicken out!"

Fast-forwarded for the sake of the narrative, the reprint from the newspaper, after the first broadcast on the radio:

Portrait of an Impossible Relationship
Minute Dramolet
by Rainer B.

Persons:	*Father*
	Son
Location	*Open space*
Time	*Present*

Father and son racing, panting, breathing heavily

Father	Stop
	Do not run away
Son	So that you catch me
	Put me in a cage
	As your dancing bear
	Force me to dance
	According to your mood
Father	I only want your best
	No harm
	No more nonsense
	Stop and listen to me
	I have begotten you
Son	Ha ha ha

	I jerk off into my hand
	Stretch out my hand towards you
	"Here you have your stake back"
	And we're even forever and ever -
	The bit of semen you had squirted
	to your pleasure
	Creates no we
Father	Unseemly how you speak to your father
Son	Plain language
Father	And this shall be my son
Son	*laughing* I wish I wasn't

The father falls down.

Son	*terrified, crying out in deepest sorrow*
	Wake up wake up wake up
	Stop this stupid game
	Your game is not funny at all -
	Ah there you are again
Father	*Chop-chop Prussian*
	What comes to your mind
	Did you embrace me
	In public
	That all people notice this feminine behaviour

The End

The wheel of time turned back a few turns. Time again before the mini radio play text is in print in the newspaper and the play is broadcast.

The proud father wants to do well in any case. In his meeting in the lodge building in Aarau, he sets the alarm on his wristwatch to exactly one minute before the broadcast of his son's minute drama is over. As soon as his watch beeps, he excuses himself from the meeting for a moment. Runs to the nearest phone. Puts in the son's number. Catches him. From the background noise at the son's, he realizes that the son is celebrating in big company. The father effusively congratulates the son on his success and says how proud he is of him.

"Tank you. How did you like the play," the son asks with a strangely uncertain undertone in his voice.

"Your short radio play must have been excellent. Otherwise the radio station wouldn't have accepted, produced and broadcast it."

"What do you think of the play? I mean, your oppinion of it."

"To be honest, I am at a meeting ..."

"Then the congratulations and your enthusiasm don't refer to my work, just to the fact that I made it to the radio?! And this from you, who always had taught me, never to show off with things you I don't know and believe!"

The son is most irritated. The father tries to justify himself. What normally would have ended in a wild argument und loud screams, fades away in a quiet goodbye. Father and son are equally outraged by the way the other communicates. The friends of the son congratulate him to his thoughtful father, who seems to be so enthusiastic about his son's writing. Another, taciturn, fight in the shadow.

In Brugg, the father stands in front of the display of a jewellery shop and looks at the beautiful pieces. Suddenly he percieves a voice. From behind his back. Did somebody address him? He is startled and turns around. He looks in the face of a young man, who is standing behind him and whom he does not know. The young man stares in a particular way at him. Then utters hesitatingly, "Don't you recognize me?", and shows a puzzled face.

Only then does the penny drop. The father could slap himself, for not immediately having recognized his own son.

„You surely know, that you and Mummy expect me for lunch today. When my train from Zurich entered the Brugg Station Area I perceived through the window of my waggon, how you are strolling home on the main street in Brugg to have lunch at home. I thought, if I start to run immediately after having left the train, I can catch up with you and we can walk home together …"

Then they both shake their heads and laugh about it.

The father, a coin collector by passion, discovers a gold coin Westphalian Peace 1648, after the 30 Years War, at a coin dealer. The son is thirty-eight. Their father-son quarrels, their shadow fights, their war now lasts a good 30 years, so peace is due. The father buys the coin and gives it to the son as a Christmas present, expecting the son to take the hint. The son politely thanks the father for the gift and also briefly asks him what the historical significance of the coin is, but does not seem to recognize the irony behind the gift. Instead, the son gives his father a richly illustrated paperback book about the German painter Caspar David Friedrich under the same Christmas tree. "Because you like Caspar David Friedrich so much!"

The father does not like to pretend. He thanks the son politely. Then he goes to one of his many book racks, pulls out the same pretty paperback picture book and tells the son, "You already gave me the same picture book last year." The son is terribly embarrassed. Then father and son laugh about it and toast each other with champagne.

The son is still without a decent job. He works as a private secretary for an architect and an emeritus university professor and as a photo model for an agency, hoping for his breakthrough as a writer. During a visit home, he approaches his father with a request to support him with an amount equivalent to approximatively three months' wages. So that he can work fulltime on his new theatre play. In the present situation he can't really concentrate on his literary work. He wishes time to write in peace, without the annoying stress with all his various jobs. He is convinced, that he is on the verge of a breakthrough as a writer. He talks to dramaturges at various theatres. The father is somehow puffed, that his son comes to him with this request, but finds the request totally out of line. If he wants to be an artist, he should see for himself how he gets on. At the same time, he doesn't want to scare him away, now that the son obviously has finally gained some trust in him, his father. A ruse spontaneously occurs to him. The father looks at the son with a thoughtful look and raises to a short speech.

"I would like to help you out. As you know, I came here to Switzerland as a refugee. In Germany, I and my family lost everything. I have always taken good care of you, my family. Mummy and I were able to afford this terrace house. But, I regret, I have no savings. I am not in a position to give you an amount equal to three months' wages, just like that."

The father notices how impressed the son is. The father is somewhat embarrassed that the son exuberantly emphasizes, how he especially appreciates his, the father's, openness ad now can talk about the difficult times he has been through. Then the son turns to Mummy. With the same request. As he knows, has her own assets, manages them herself and is not really poor.

"I think it's ridiculous for a fully grown man of over thirty years to still have to beg for money!", is her clear answer.

The father is amazed at the harshness and consistency of his Little Monster. He can understand that the son is shocked by Mummy's harsh attitude. But at the same time laughs to himself that he, the father, and his Little Monster take the same directions without consultation.

A little later, the daughter announces that she and her husband are thinking of buying a terrace house. Father and Mummy congratulate her on their decision. They ask her, if she and her husband would appreciate a financial contribution for the purchase of the house. The daughter is overwhelmed and most delighted. Mummy and father consult together. They decide, that each of them gives the young couple with the toddler an amount equal to twenty-one months' wages. A deal is signed.

Some days later, the phone rings and Mummy answers it. To her astonishment the son calls. He never does it out of the blue. Moreover he sounds stressed. Wishes to talk immediately to his father. Is not willing to chat with her at all. A puzzlinh behaviour. Mummy hands the phone to the father. Who is most surprised, that the son wants to talk to him on the phone. This has never occured so far. The son sounds calm and collected.

"Father, Bettina just called me and told me, that you ans Mummy are helping her to buy a house. She also told me, how much money you and Mummy give her. That's wonderful. I really do appreciate it. Don't interrupt me, please! Typical that you have quite a lot of money, to support accumulation of wealth, but no money to support a poor artist in the family. That's not the point for me. . I am deeply disappointed. That you won't give me the money is okay. But the fact, that you were giving me a maudlin story, a lie, to justify your refusal, to give me some money, and that I believed you and felt ashamed, not to have considered this, hits me hard. I never can trust you again. As a father you are dead to me me. From now on you count for me as anyone else. Our relationship will be nive on the surface, but basically non-committal. I can no longer seriously trust you. Goodbye.".

Before the father can start with his apologies, admitting that his lie was a foolish one, that he deeply regrets, the son has finished the call. The following day, the father transfers an amount equivalent to four and a half months' wages to the bank account of his son. Three days later the son calls home. The phone call again is answered by Mummy. The son asks to speak to his father. The son politely thanks the father for the money and ends the call. As much as the father regrets and reproaches himself, he admires the son for his courage to be outspoken, which alone creates clear conditions in difficult situations.

The father has stomach pains. As a doctor, he takes painkillers by self-medication. The pain does not subside. He eats more painkillers. The pain becomes unbearable. His Little Monster is worried and drives him to their family doctor. The doctor admits the father to hospital as an emergency. Emergency operation. Burst appendix. The operation is successful. The father is still a little weak. Lying in the hospital bed. Knock on the room door. The father calls softly, "Come in". After the door has opened, the son tentatively enters the hospital room through the door frame and closes the door behind him. The father can hardly believe his eyes. His son is visiting him! The father is pleased. The son seems intimidated by this surrounding and the sight he has.

"Tough luck, my son. Your old man does not bite the dust so quickly. Too early to inherit from me," the father grumbles out and straightens up in bed: With difficulty. Obviously to get out of bed. Sits down on the edge of the bed opposite the window. Sstands up on wobbly legs. Until he realizes that he is wearing a hospital nightgown: That is open at the back. The two parts of the gown only held together by a small piece of clothing at the back of his neck. He feels the two pieces of fabric flutter apart when he stands up. It flashes through his mind, that presents unintentionally and indecently his naked backside to his son. The son, who is still standing by the door, sees from him, the father, who is now standing, the almost naked back and the completely exposed buttocks. The sluggishly hanging arse cheeks of an old man. Who struggles to hold himself upright on wobbly legs. The father turns as quickly as he can and, in slight pain at the surgical wound, slumps into the armchair standing beside the bed. He just notices the son's aghast look, which turns from the height of the father's previously visible naked bottom to his, the father's, now visible face. With a smile. The father is embarrassed that the son sees him in this state and like this.

"Nice of you to come and see me."

"I thought I'd stop by."

"After all, you took the trip from Zurich to Brugg specifically to see your old man in hospital."

Later, the father confesses to the mother that however one reacts, one always reacts wrongly.

"I explode. Afterwards, I'm wiser. Know, I shouldn't have exploded. And yet, the misplaced explosion has brought a purification. Ah, my dear Little Monster, life is most complex!"

"The shadow fights, Hansel, are over. You're reconciled ..."

"No, we're not. He and me still tend to shadow fights. A fight is a fight. We two are facing each other with contradictory positions. We have fought for decades. We have never avoided an argument and an arising fight. To avoid it, would have been a declaration of bankruptcy. The opponent would not have been worth fighting with. He and I always have considered the other one worth fighting with. Perhaps - an adventurous explanation - because reconciliation is so important to both of us. To him and to me. I hated him and I love him, this fool of a son, despite or precisely because he is such a fool. But we just can't hug each other. No physical contact. I am Prussian. We are doomed to haunt each other cerebrally. Pure cynicism and satire. And not be able to get away from each other."

THE SON AND THE GHOST OF HIS FATHER

11.

You write in your diary on March 29, 1985:

Yesterday, between ten and a quarter past, my father was hit by a tree, a beech, in the Brugg Forest . At five past twelve, he died in the Brugg District Hospital. During his morning walk he met father and son M., farmers from Lauffohr, who were cutting wood. He exchanged a few words with the father, then with the son, who was fiddling with a small beech tree with a diameter of only about 25 cm. When the son went back to work, my father went on. The former saw, that the latter was heading directly under the falling tree, called after him, tried to deflect the fall of the tree, to delay it ... arm, leg and pelvis fractures on one side and a crushed rib cage, which was then probably also the cause of death because of the associated breathing difficulties. At half past one, I got the news by phone from my sister Bets. Bets and Jörg picked me up to drive to Umiken. Now, with the death of my father has happend, what I dreaded. Mourning? I scan what has happened for symbolic aspects: Violent death. In the forest. He strolls absent minded past the barrier, marked with visible ribbons, in the direction of a falling tree, cut down by a young woodcutter. .Didn't great-grandfather Gustav (a medical mishap) and grandfather Eugen (heart attack in desolate times) already die not - quite -

natural deaths. I breathe a sigh of relief. The relief is,
that everything has passed so painlessly so far. …

The father looses his life and becomes a spook in your head. The shadow fights between him and you are definitely over, aren't they!

You are afraid to play the role of the grieving son in front of your relatives, friends and acquaintances.

In the Neue Zürcher Zeitung, the headline "Retired doctor killed by tree in the Brugg Forest" appears under the heading "Accidents and crimes", followed by a short article.

You hated your father. So be it! And at the end, a favourite saying of your father's is added with a wink and a grin: ‚Such is life!'

12.

You should have put behind your former statement, that the shadow fights between your father and you were definitely over, instead of an exclamation mark a question mark. Your father's death cannot at once make your father complex disappear.

Your mother asks you to help her remove the now superfluous bed from her bedroom. She needs to have air to breathe again. She asks you, if you would mind if she donated all of your father's clothes, most of which were still excellent and some of which were new, to the Königsfelden Clinic. Bettina already has agreed. In addition, your mother asks you to take care of the tons of papers that your father had hoarded in his study and in two cupboards in the closet room that were filled to bursting point. To dispose of the stuff as you please. Bettina and she had no interest in these papers.

Spontaneously flashes through your mind, typical of my father, blindly collecting everything that comes under his eyes. Keeps it safeguarded. And now I, the son, am supposed to take care of all this crap! At the same time your curiosity is waked up and the prospect of delving in your father's so meticulously hidden papers at your whim is itching you.

While you go through your fathers papers, he mutates from the hated person to this young man in exile who comes to Switzerland in 1937 to write a doctoral thesis. He has to realize that there can be no going back to Germany. Survives with dignity through charm, grit and coquetry. He finds fulfilment in his job and family, with his long-awaited son and descendent. But this is the beginning of new difficulties that add up to the difficulties with his refugee status. The thrilling story of survival thanks to the will not to perish.

You learn things about your father's life that you hadn't known. Little by little, you gain distance from the picture you had made of him. You feel ashamed that you had so far ignored his real personality and endlessly fought with him. He resurrects as an independent new man. You want to ask him a thousand questions. Too late. His portrait condenses in you into a fictional novel and a homage to this man, whom you had perceived one-sidedly during his lifetime and who had remained unknown to you as an indept person. Forget about remorse and a guilty conscience ! The shadow fights are finally over!

The reappraisal of the history of your father and his German family occupies you for over two decades. This occupation results in a five-volume work, 'Privatzeug 1856-2012. Versuch einer Spurensuche' (Private matters 1856-2012. An attempt to find traces). Each volume consists partly of documents. 'Spur 1 Reisen' (Trace 1 Travels): Letters from your grandmother, persecuted in Germany, to your father in Switzerland between 1937 and 1944. ,Spur 3 Schreiben' (Trace 3 To write)': Diary 1869 to 1872 of a great-grandmother from an emancipated Jewish family in Schlesien, which she began as a 16-year-old in 1868. ‚Spur 4 Dichten' (Trace 4 To write poetry): Poetry collection ‚Ein Glaubensbekenntnis' (A confession of faith) by your father from 1934, referring to Ferdinand Freiligrath's political poetry collection of the same title from 1844. ‚Spur 5 Weben' (Trace 5 To wave): Letters from relatives and friends of your father, who remained in Germany or are scattered all over the world to your father from 1945 to 1956. ‚Spur 2 Spielen' (Trace 2 To play) contains only quotations from the documents used in the other volumes and is the most personal and intimate outflow of your playful approach to the partly dramatic family history in the form of a radio play and a theatre play.

You decide to donate all the papers, documents, scientific and fiction manuscripts inherited from your father to the ‚Institut für Zeitgeschichte der ETH Zürich' (Institute for Contemporary History), who is most interested in it. The tidying up work is done. During the lifetime you shared with your father, both of you had made your relationship most difficult. Now it is all over. And the traces of your father will be preserved for posterity.

With your meticulous processing of your father's life story, you have given him back his dignity. That finally settles the issue for you, doesn't it!

13.

Theoretically the chapter of your father is closed for you. Sure! You no longer bear a grudge against your father. You made peace with him

‚Weit gefehlt, ihr Männer von Athen!' (Far from it, men of Athens!), a favourite quoting by Platon of your humanist educated father.

In your publications, you made no secret of the fact that you had hated your father.Which is understandable, as he had never appreciated you enough. Had mocked you and always put you down. No praise. The confession of your hatred has been liberating to you. Now slowly something like a bad conscience creeps in. What the heck about feelings of guilt! Both of you survived. That is to say, your father passed away. Not because of your hatred. But due to an accident. What's over, is over. No more endless shadow fights. They had taken place in the shadow. And what of the past had been allowed to appear in the light, had been quite good, after all.

Well, well, well, beware! Your father's ghost is ready to haunt you. Watch out! You make a grinning face. 'What can a ghost do to me!'

The ghost will catch you, where you expect it least. Announced by a rumbling in your head and a trivial situation.

A quoting slips mockingly in your mind.
'Who is it?'

An ironic laugh escapes you. The Shakespeare quoting from Hamlet. You know, you don't have to avenge an injustice. Instead of brushing up your Shakespeare and realize, how eternally right and true he is, you laugh. Don't push away the ghost. Ask, when he, this ghost or clown, knocks on your brains, who he is! Hamlet and his father, oh! You vaguely remember a performance of Peter Ustinov's play 'Photo Finish. An Adventure in Biography in Three Acts' in the Schauspielhaus Zurich beginning of the sixties. In this play a son and his father - what had they had together? Shadow fights, nothing but shadow fights. Help, help, help, sons and their fathers ! You're over it by now. You can easily say,'My father has been, after all, okay. Maybe I would have wanted to love him and to be loved by him.'

The Kunsthaus Zurich is showing the exhibition 'Bilderwahl! Reformation' (Choise of Paintings. Reformation). Visiting this exhibition will distract you. Bans obsessive thinking. Creates distance. Shows that next to your small world there is a big, wide world. That offers you other things, than these dreary domestic problems, where people get on each other's nerves in a space, too limited to escape.

Gottfried Keller, the famous Swiss writer from the 19th century, is mentioned in the exhibition as an important innovator in the 19th century. The famous portrait of the famous Gottfried Keller by the famous Swiss painter Karl Stauffer is shown in the exhibition. This successful porträt of Keller is always an eye catcher. It touches you. It also stirs up memories of your grandfather from Oberrohrdorf.

The memory of Grandfather from Oberrohrdorf is linked to Gottfried Keller and his novella ‚Das Fähnlein der sieben Aufrechten' (The flag of the seven upright – the upright in the novel is a group of friends, who all are marksmen) from 1860, as your family legend goes. Following this legend Grandfather, an avid marksman, had entered the festival arena at the ‚Eidgenössischen Schützenfest' (Federal Shooting Festival) in Aarau 1924 together with a group of fellow marksmen as the 'Fähnlein der sieben Aufrechten'. The group had recieved enthusiastic and memorable applause. Grandfather had since then attached the designation 'one of the seven upright'. When you first got to know, why Grandfather was called by several people, ‚one of the seven uright' you realized that this name was due to Gottfried Kellers novella. You then were obsessed with Brecht, Camus and above all French authors, later also John Irving and Kurt Vonnegut jr. from the USA. Keller clearly fell short in your consciousness. Only later you were tempted to read Gottfried Keller's novella 'Das Fähnlein der sieben Aufrechten'. The well and grippingly written story about a group of marksmen, who were close friends, linked to a Romeo and Julia story, touches you. You marvel at how Keller, as a keen observer, can realistically capture how people from different backgrounds react to each other and get along together. And the love story with a happy ending to boot! At a Federal Shotting Festival in the 19th century! These memories come to your mind, while you are looking at the Keller-Portrait in the Kunsthaus Zurich.

Right next to the Keller portrait hangs another portrait. The portrait of a man. This portrait catches your eye. You like the man depicted. You like to look at him as he is depicted. Even facial features. An averted gaze directed at something specific outside the picture. Could be a hipster of today. Caption: 'Unknown (around Gottfried Schadow). Portrait of August Follenius, c. 1825/1830. Oil on canvas. Kunsthaus Zurich, gift of Miss Susanna Vogt, 1948. The German political emigrant August Follenius supported Gottfried Keller in his early days as a writer. The two liberals defended the faith in the ‚Zürcher Atheismusstreit' (Zurich fight of atheism) of 1846. Critics of confessional Swiss patriotism declared atheism to be a prerequisite for political freedom. Follenius countered Keller, who spread the unifying love of faith, with the infinite, which 'moves the spirit'.'

The name Follenius / Follen sends alarm bells ringing in your head. Your father had worked for years on an essay about Follen and researched his life. When he started this work end of the 30th or beginning of the 40th he wrote to your grandmother in Breslau about his undertaking. Grandmother wrote back in a letter, 'And now, to my shame, I must confess to you that I know nothing at all about a lost poet, A.L. Follen. When and where did he live, and why did you come across him? In any case, good luck to work.' And in a later letter, 'My beloved boy. ... Now, through your hints, I am also somewhat oriented about the poet A.L. Follen. He must have been a strange saint - at any rate an original, or shall we say a crazy chicken? Did he play a certain role, or did he clearly stand out because of his peculiarities?' A few years later your father published a paper on Follenius, also Follen (August Adolf Ludwig Follen, 1794 to 1855). You are spontaneously pricked by curiosity about what your father might have found in this Follen. You remember having hold the periodical, in which your fathers paper has been publised, in your hands while occupied with your father's documents. Too bad, that you have given all of your father's documents to the ‚Archiv der Zeitgeschichte'. The documents have not yet been processed to such an extent, that they can be accessed.

Your curiosity spurs you to follow up your fathers essay on Follen. You make a pilgrimage to the 'Kantonsbibliothek Aargau' (Cantonal Library Aargau) in Aarau. In the catalogue of the library you find your father's name listed with several works. And you even discover : 'Bressler, Hans Günther. The Late Romantic A. A. L. Follen in Psychiatric View: Outlines of an Unpublished Pathography'.

You are reading at a table in the reading room. Bent over the yellowed pages of an old periodical. You understand, that your father came across Follen through Herwegh and Freiligrath while studying the lives of German refugees in Switzerland in the 19th century. Follen had been persecuted in Germany, had to leave his fatherland, came to Switzerland, married a Swiss woman, became Swiss himself, worked as a teacher and politician and, among other things, influenced Swiss writers. Obviously such a biografie had appealed to your father. Then you nearly can't believe what you read ....

> *... Besides the undeniable craving for recognition, we believe in a defiant neurosis planted at an early*

age and originally directed against the father, which subsequently ran up against all authority. The father never ostracized him enough, later sneered at him, and the favourite brother was a neurotic anyway. Now August sees in any lawful restriction the hand of the father against which he must rebel. With his poor studies he punishes his producer, just as with his waste of money and his debts, for everything is paid by the latter. ...

... His lack of criticism, his alienation from the world, his obstinacy and maladjustment correspond to the image of schizoidism. Our schizoid neurotic overthrows his father along with all ruling power, but transposes the relationship in an infantile manner and becomes an emperor by his own grace.

The inner causes of August's revolutionary attitude nevertheless contradict his aristocratising personality and ultimately appear inauthentic. This makes August in this the mouthpiece of the more active brother, for whose superiority he avenges himself with orgies of fantasy. Finally, the peculiar structure of August's circle of friends and his sheer antifeminine attitude speak for homoerotic tendencies. .. All in all, we would like to describe the man Follen towards the end of his second Zurich period as a schizoid, submaniform psychopath with pseudological, hysteria-like and querulous traits as well as homoerotic aspirations, which are still based in the early neurotically processed childhood experiences.

Hans Günther Bressler, Der Spätromantiker A. A. L. Follen in psychiatrischer Schau: Grundzüge einer unveröffentlichten

Pathographie, in Schweizerische Medizinische Wochenschrift No. 37, 1949, pp. 867 ff.

Before and after your, the son's, birth, your father had struggled with a highly problematic father-son relationship. Analyses. Pathologizes the son. Clearly recognizes the mistakes of that father in dealing with his son.

The morning after your visit to the library in Aarau, you record the following dream in your diary:

> *In the parlour in our flat in the main building in Königsfelden. We enter the parlour, Father in front, me behind. We are both relaxed, easy-going and in a good mood. Father walks towards the window that looks out onto the forecourt. As he does so, he lets slip that he hasn't had a chance to read my book (Trace 1 Travels) yet. I now hold the book in my hands and point out to him that it could also be of great interest to him, because I use excerpts from his diary in it. Not to mention that the design of the book is ingenious. Suddenly, it occurs to me that I haven't told Father at all, that I've sent the documents to the Archives of Contemporary History. That's when I wake up. When I wake up, I think to myself that Father has died and that I can't tell him about my published books, containing the family history and, above all, his documents and diaries.*

14.

You fetch the small broom and shovel from the cleaning cupboard in the kitchen. Finally, after days of making wide circles around the pile of broken pieces on the floor of your study, you clean up the remains of the fallen and shattered Harpocrates figure. With a somehow guilty conscience. Rremove the broken pieces and dirt from the floor at the point of impact of the figure and in the vicinity of the circles drawn by the individual fragments at the moment of shattering. The Harpocrates figure, antique, Greek, made of clay, had been bought by your father in an antique shop ages ago. He had been terribly proud of this genuine antiquity. After your father's death, no one had wanted it. You took it. Not out of affection. Just so as not to let the precious piece go to waste. Now it lies in pieces before you. And you are armed with a small broom and a small shovel.

You cannot defend yourself against your gaze, which is suddenly attracted by what you perceive as a paltry thing. A barely perceptible, but nevertheless catching your eye, pretty dust lichen on one of the shards, flickering slightly in your breath as it penetrates it. Trembling as if about to take off. Fine, slightly iridescent in the bright daylight streaming into the room from outside. You look around you. You look at all the things that have fallen to you in the course of your life and, for lack of a further purpose, have ended up on your various racks as dust catchers, as you realize only now for the first time. You blow on the things. Dust swirls up. Immediately you have to sneeze. You are involuntarily reminded of your dust allergy. The dust must go!

You shake your wise head. That you had to reach old age before you became aware of the fact that things gather dust. This realization does not shake you. You still feel perfectly comfortable in your skin. But this realization kicks your mind. The cleaning lady who had cleaned your house for twenty years until six weeks ago moves back to her home country, Portugal. She finds a successor, also from Portugal, who will start work next week. You sense an opportunity to end your habit of running away from the cleaning lady. The previous cleaning lady did everything she could to keep Monsieur's study, as she called you, spotlessly clean. You sat there like on pins and needles until she said to you the redeeming words, "Monsieur, j'ai fini dans votre chambre!" (Sir, I have finished in your study). You kept dropping, "Why does she always spend hours cleaning my study!" To which you were met with the reply of your wife, "Don't exaggerate and don't get hysterical every time she spends ten minutes vacuuming and dusting in your study."

You decide to dust yourself from now on. The new cleaning lady will be instructed only to vacuum your study briefly. The dusting will be done by the Monsieur himself. Humming a happy tune, you start dusting, picking up every item that is gathering dust on the countless cover plates of the countless racks in your study and dusting thoroughly. Until, to your surprise, dusk falls outside. You realize with horror that you've been dusting for over three hours ! And you haven't finished yet! You sigh, if there wasn't junk everywhere, if the cover plates of the racks were empty, you would have dusted in a few seconds. And already the decision jumps into your head, the stuff has to go!

One's possessions, oh! All these things ! You exactly know, where all these things came from. Gotten as gifts, inherited or bought by yourself. You own them all. And now they are standing uselessly around. You keep all these things, because you're accostumed to them. You keep them out of an insane respect for the donor, the testator. To be honest, you don't give a shit whether you own these things or not. Some of the objects are valuable and precious. Others are just kitschy and worthless. Never or no more longing for them or sensual stimulus by them. You feel light and liberated by imagining, that you will get rid of all these things and how you will have room to breathe in your study. No more superfluous antique furniture, candlesticks, statues, knick-knacks, porcelain objects, where they are not needed! Your obsession instinct to collect and accumulate makes you laugh. Your father had had the same obsession. You inherited it from him. Together with all the things in your study from his estate. Sure, some pieces tell or are connected to nice stories and memories. So what, the stories and memories are either in your conscience or not, with or without all material things. And if they fall in the black hole of memory, they only do what so many things do. Much less ballast.

Stubborn as you are - you inherited as well your stubbornness from your father - something you set into your mind, has to be tackled and carried through. After the pretty antique Harpocrates figure has gone down the drain by chance and has passed away and turned to dust without you having to shed a tear for it, let alone miss it, you hawk freshly, freely and cheerfully in shops and on Internet portals what is in your way and breathe a sigh of relief when the clearing-out operation is successfully completed. You can book a financial profit. You are left with only a few, unremarkable items, which you put into a rubbish bag. You say goodbye to the bag and throw it secretly at night into a rubbish bin in your neighbourhood.

What remains are memories and stories. Pretty, contradictory, amusing stories that fill entire books, which are not reality, but references to events that were or could have been like this, but also completely different. Part of a novel in progress.

Please don't underestimate that your father and your entire environment opened the way for you to books, to art, to the theatre, to writing, to social commitment. Please do not underestimate that your father involuntarily modelled independence without sentimentality as a survival strategy for you, and that you involuntarily copied and adopted it from him. Do not underestimate the most lasting after-effects of your father, whom you once hated so much, but now enjoy portraying, in your everyday life today. Even after his death his ghost guides you to three men, who became your friends and whom you do not want to miss.

More than ten years after your father's death, a letter, still addressed to your late father, flutters into your parents' pretty terrace house, which is now occupied by your mother, the widow. Your mother calls to tell you, that a historian from Germany, who is researching the life and her refugee fate from Breslau to London of your father's cousin Hilde G., who recently had died in London. He asks for informations about Hilde G.. He had come across the address of your father in Hilde G.'s papers. And he assumes, that your father as a close relative to Hilde G. has a lot of information about her life and fate. You take over. You contact the historian, who lives in the German Lake Constance region near the Swiss border. You tell him, that your father had died. But you could give him informations on Hilde G. as well. You visit him at his home. You hit it off right away. You have become best friends for over twenty years now. At every meeting, you and Christian F. toast to Hilde G., who brought you together.

This story of a friendship founded posthumously by your father veers into an earlier side-story that you find so delicious and which shows you figuratively, how intricate the paths of history and stories sometimes are. You remember how Aunt Hilde G., who had been a successful paediatrician in London, was still a good match in her old age, when she married her partner of many years, a successful engineer. He died before her. Hilde G. died shortly after your father. After Hilde G. had died, her executor of the will, an employee of a bank in London, had had written a litter to your late father. He knows from personal papers of Hilde G., that your father is a close relative of her. He asks for your father's help in finding Hilde G.'s legal heirs of her widespread family. He also mentiones, that the estate is considerable. This letter ends up with you. You contact this executor of the will. So far no last will of Hilde G. has been found. So the legal succession comes into play. You draw up a family tree for him. You realize, that you and your family belong to the legal heirs. Your heart leaps for joy, great expectations to finally become unexpectedly a rich man. But then the executor of the will informs you that finally a will has been found, in which Hilde G. disposes of her entire estate and excludes the legal heirs. You take the sad news in your stride. You explain to the executor that you, as a person interested in family history, have a wish. Hilde G. had, when leaving Germany, certainly taken family papers and documents with her to England. These papers were today worthless to third parties. But they interest you very much. Whether it would be possible to pass on these family papers to you, despite the fact that you have lost the quality of heir. The executor explains that he would be happy to do so. There had indeed been papers among the belongings of Hilde G., but they had been disposed of elsewhere, when the flat was vacated and were now no longer available. You have no choice but to shrug your shoulders in equanimity. After all, it could have been. End of this side-story.

And back to Christian F.. You are dying to know from him, how he came across Hilde G. as his subject of research. He laughs. It were pure coincidence. He and his wife had a soft spot for England. They often travelled to England. On the occasion of such a trip, they just had under an hour, before they had to leave for the airport after checking out of the hotel. Because they were both book freaks, they had rummaged around in bookshops and antiquarian bookshops on Charing Cross Road. In an antiquarian bookshop, he made a find that piqued his curiosity. Lying under a table on a pile of books. A package wrapped in brown wrapping paper and tied tightly, with the inscription 'German papers from between the wars'. He immediately asked the antiquarian bookseller present in the shop what the papers tied up in the parcel were about and whether he could open the parcel briefly. The man apologized. He was just a friend of the owner of the antiquarian bookshop and was keeping an eye on the shop because the owner had to leave on urgent business. The owner would be back in a few minutes. He could not and did not want to decide anything. How much did the package cost? If there was no price written on it, he had no idea. Christian F. made it clear to the man that he had no time to wait and was on his way to Heathrow. Meanwhile, he waved what appeared to be a large enough bank note to convince the man that he could probably hand over the parcel without incurring the displeasure of his friend, the owner of the shop. And Christian F. bought a pig in a poke. The pig in the poke turned out to be old papers concerning a family from Germany, mainly Breslau, having belonged to a certain Hilde G.. Christian F. laughingly explains that it was these papers that first led him to Hilde G., the subject of his research. And because one of the most recent addresses in the pile of papers had been your father's address and because he was determined to continue his research ...

So by pure chance you got hold of the very papers, that had escaped from Hilde G.'s inheritance in London and were found by a fellow writer, who became your friend ...

The second friendship founded posthumously by your father begins for you at a social event. You are invited to the retirement party of a former colleague, who works in a different office than you, but with whom you had been in frequent and friendly contact. As chance would have it, you find yourself at a large table, where among many other people two persons living in the Canton Aargau are sitting. You originate from Kanton Aargau. Everybody at your table is most surprised, when you tell them, that as a child and an adolescent you had lived in the Psychiatric

Clinic Königsfelden, as your father had been a doctor there. A man who still lives in Kölliken, Canton Aargau, but works in Zürich, asks you, whether you know, since you grew up in Königsfelden, if the story, that a doctor at the clinic once had had a love affair with a female patient at the clinic, is true or not. You have never heard anything about such a story. Therefore, you cannot answer the question. The man then explains, that a Swiss writer, who also lives in Kölliken, had written a novel about just such an affair in Königsfelden. He was terribly curious to know, whether the story of the novel was based on facts or made up. The author was Ernst Strebel. The title of the novel is 'Ein Letztes noch' (One Last Thing).

This information is intriguing you. Your are curious. Some days later you buy the book. You devour it with excitement and pleasure. The novel is about the Swiss writer Conrad Ferdinand Meyer and his stay as a patient in the Psychiatric Clinic Königsfelden in 1892/3, and tells on the side of the affair between a doctor at the clinic and a female patient of the clinic. You are enthusiastic about the novel. You write to the author, how much you liked the novel and how well he succeeded in describing the atmosphere of Königsfelden, which you know very well because you grew up there. Ernst S. contacts you by return of post. You arrange to meet in Königsfelden under the large plane tree in front of the Old Hospital. You immediately get along perfectly well. You learn from Ernst S. that he has come across the stay of Meyer in Königsfelden as well as the actually documented affair between a doctor of the clinic and a patient of the clinic in the book published for the centenary of new buildings of the modern Königsfelden Clinic, written by your father!.

Once again, your father posthumously acted as a matchmaker and unintentionally played chance in forging your friendship with fellow writer Ernst Strebel.

While studying the documents from your father's estate, the diaries, the letters, and then while working on your book 'Spur 1 Reisen' (Trace 1 Travels), which tells of your father's arrival in Switzerland and his first time in Königsfelden, you come across the name of a colleague of your father's with whom he is on friendly terms, as can be seen from the frequently mentioned joint undertakings in your fathers diaries. The friend's name is Boris Pritzker. Pritzker had started a family somewhat earlier than your father. In one of your father's diaries from 1947 you read, 'Frau Doktor Pritzker and Gret met with both their children for coffee and cake'. So, you had played with Pritzker children without being able to remember. The name Pritzker had always been familiar to you from your parents' stories. Then you remember a vague perception. A son of Boris Pritzker had somehow been involved in the staging of the dramatic implementation of a research by Boris Pritzker about the search for a hangman for the last execution in Switzerland. In the Swiss Writers Lexikon is listed an Andreas Pritzker, born one day after you, who's father is Boris Pritzker. When your 'Spur 1 Reisen' is published, you send Andreas Pritzker a copy of the book. Mentioning, that his father appeared prominently in your father's diary, excerpts of which are reproduced in the book. Soon afterwards you meet. 67 years after you had played together as toddlers, you fall into each other's arms like old acquaintances. Fellow writer Andreas Pritzker is your friend from then on.

Your father's ghost says goodbye! Is gone! Goodbye shadow fights! Your supposed hatred for your father has melted away and turns out to have been a longing for his love in disguise.

Nevertheless, countless good and bad memories of your father flash up again and again. Imposing themselves on you. No longer disturbing. But uplifting. In the intimate vividness of a fictional narrative, a novel beyond all biographical facts, they create in you the need to give a face to the person who had been your father and thus to approach the true character that he had been from the most diverse perspectives, so that by chance an approximately true-to-life portrait of your father will succeed.